The Mid-life Crisis of Morris Bridges

Ken Cooper

Copyright © 2017 Ken Cooper

All rights reserved, including the right to reproduce this book, or portions thereof in any form. No part of this text may be reproduced, transmitted, downloaded, decompiled, reverse engineered, or stored, in any form or introduced into any information storage and retrieval system, in any form or by any means, whether electronic or mechanical without the express written permission of the author.

This is a work of fiction. Names and characters are the product of the author's imagination and any resemblance to actual persons, living or dead, is entirely coincidental.

The views expressed in this work are solely those of the author and do not necessarily reflect the views of the publisher, and the publisher hereby disclaims any responsibility for them.

ISBN: 978-1-326-96234-0

Front cover designed by Steve Cooper

PublishNation
www.publishnation.co.uk

Make him laugh and he will think you a trivial fellow, but bore him in the right way and your reputation is assured.
—*W. Somerset Maugham*

Acknowledgements

Editing services provided by Alexandria Matthews at
www.proofreadingserviceuk.com

Preface

Morris Bridges was a travelling salesman in ladies' garments for the larger-sized woman. His sales area spread from Lincolnshire across to Shropshire and everywhere south of that line. He represented Squires of Harrogate, which was owned by third-generation family member Harold Squires.

Life was pretty ordinary for Morris and he accepted his lot, including the misspelling of his name. It should have been Maurice, but his parents, due to overindulging in celebratory drinks before the christening and registration, couldn't remember how to spell Maurice, and his father could only remember he drove a Morris Oxford – so that was it!

Chapter 1

Morris was a medium-built man with medium brown hair and medium aspirations. He drove a black Rover 75 and wore a pinstripe suit and bowler hat. He lived in Berkshire in a cul-de-sac called Willow Avenue. If not staying in a hotel, he would kiss his wife goodbye on the cheek every morning, pick up his briefcase and carefully reverse the Rover out of the garage of their red-brick semi-detached 1930s house.

Occasionally he would see his neighbour weeding the neat flowerbeds. They would exchange greetings along the lines of, 'Still travelling in ladies' underwear, I see,' and would fall about laughing, to which Morris would politely acknowledge, 'You are a comic, Sidney.'

Morris planned his routes meticulously each weekend covering most major towns in each county. His target customers were 'outfitters for the fashion conscious'. Morris can't recall how he got into ladies' underwear. It evolved from selling buttons, which were big in the forties and fifties until Mr Whitcomb invented the zip and all the perils that can bring. Nobody wanted buttons any more, whether they were mother-of-pearl, bone, metal or – God help us – plastic.

Then one day he read an article in the *Daily Express* that women were getting larger. He could vouch for this as Penelope, the current Mrs Bridges, was of the larger vogue, brought about by the invention of the vacuum cleaner, washing machine and tumble dryer, thus cutting out any form of exercise Mrs Bridges would have had apart from peeling the shells from peanuts.

Morris accepted his lot in 'Chez Nous' on Willow Avenue. His only break from the domestic scene was being a member of the bowls club and Assistant Secretary to the Spire Observation Group covering Berkshire, or S.O.G. – affectionately known as 'Soggies'. The other two members were chairman and secretary, and Morris had absolutely no aspirations to attain a higher posting. Their sole purpose was to observe and photograph church spires and log them in tidy leather-bound albums, noting the date of construction, how many finials and was the clock working. Equipment included an anorak, wellies, binoculars and flask due to the fact looking at a church spire for two hours becomes really thirsty work.

The bowls club was a much livelier affair with characters from all walks of life. Windy Farquhar who passed wind every time he bent down to bowl. Mrs B.A. Prendergast, local bank manager's widow, very strident and nobody knew what the 'B.A.' stood for – probably 'Big Arse' according to Nobby Clark from behind his cupped hand. Wendy Struthers married to a gynaecologist who apparently never took his work home, so she was constantly trying to impress the other male members (so to speak), but her wig had a funny way of sliding forward over her forehead when she released the bowls, which was very unbecoming. Morris played an average game and took it in his stride as a way of spending Sunday afternoons.

Penelope and Morris decided not to have any more children after Stanley. He proved a difficult birth for Morris because he was in Harrogate at the time and had to rush to Reading Infirmary just as The Archers was about to begin on Radio 4 – he never missed an evening episode.

Stanley, Penelope's choice, was an eccentric child and devious to the extent that Morris denied being his father. It came to a head when Stanley was attending St Benedict's, for boys aged eleven to fifteen, and in his last year was dismissed from academia for locking the Maths teacher in the stationery cupboard. Not a great crime in itself, but it involved Miss Tinker who was also looking for bulldog clips at the same time. When released, Miss Tinker apparently got an A+.

Stanley, or 'Stan the Man' as he was known, became a mod, which being in the 60s was something of a status symbol totally out of line with Mr and Mrs Bridges' lifestyle. Subsequently, Stanley was sent to the Isle of Wight to live with his Aunt Muriel to study food hygiene at Ventnor Laboratories. He ended up growing cannabis and making a fortune during music festivals.

As Morris drove along the country roads on his way to Telford in Shropshire he looked back over his life and came to the conclusion, after much deliberation, it was crap! But at fifty-four years old, this is as good as it gets.

Chapter 2

Whilst contemplating what it would be like to be Cliff Richard, haven't we all, sharing a bus with Una Stubbs in *Summer Holiday*, he was suddenly confronted with a young lady standing next to a car waving him down. Normally Morris had an inbuilt dislike for hitchhikers, but this was different – she was obviously in a predicament, and pretty.

Morris slowed down and leant across to wind down the passenger window.

The young lady leant forward into the car. She was slightly distressed that the car had broken down and was on her way to become a nurse at Telford Hospital twenty miles down the road.

'Hello, which way you going?' she asked.

This seemed pretty obvious to Morris, but under the circumstances he politely indicated the same direction as her.

Morris's mind wandered to when he was lost in Sussex once and stopped to ask a local the best way to Chichester.

'You're in it – a car,' replied the man.

'I mean, which road is the quickest?'

'Depends how fast you go.'

'Could you point me in the right direction?'

'Well, I wouldn't start from here for a start. But if you go back to the high street, I could tell you from there.'

'OK,' said Morris, somewhat exasperated, 'jump in.'

'Oh, no thanks, I've just been there.'

Morris drove off with the screeching of tyres in any direction away from the man.

He brought his senses back to the present. With the excitement of helping a young lady, Morris felt a rush of blood as he said, 'Have you got any luggage?'

'Yes, in the car.'

Morris, being a gentleman, alighted from his car and went around the back of the battered Ford Popular. There on the back seat were four large bags and a budgie in a cage.

The boot of his car was full of large size knickers with double gussets, so he squeezed the young lady's luggage onto the back seat.

After they both climbed in the car, Morris pulled away, window down, arm resting on the sill, tie had somehow become a little looser, and he put on his sunglasses. Wow – he was suddenly James Dean!

'This is very kind of you to put yourself out for me,' she said.

'It's no problem,' he answered.

'What do you do?' she asked.

Morris hesitated before replying, 'I deal in protective clothing for astronauts.' *Bloody hell,* he thought, *where did that come from?* He then added, 'And I work for the government.'

'Gosh, interesting stuff! Do you travel much?'

'Just finished a trip to Tucson in Arizona where they... No, I'm not supposed to tell,' said Morris.

'Oh, go on, I won't tell a soul.'

'Well, we've been testing spacesuits for a trip to the moon.'

'Bloody hell, we're going to the moon?' she said inquisitively.

'Soon, but keep it quiet.'

Morris never told a lie, had no reason to, but he was enjoying himself and it gave him a rush.

'Beats dealing with overweight patients and changing their bed sheets.'

'I'm sure you will be very good at it,' said Morris.

The Rover had a radio, but it was permanently tuned to Radio 4. She was no more than twenty-two years old. *How do I get the light programme or whatever it is for pop music?* He twiddled the knobs and found what he thought was pop music. It turned out to be Radio Morocco; not quite what he had in mind.

'Could you find some beat music?' he said serenely, thinking he was impressing her.

'Actually, I like the classical genre myself. My father was a conductor.'

'Buses or trains?' said Morris.

'Music – I play the piano when at home.'

'Ah yes, I like a bit of Liberace myself.' *Probably not the best way of putting it*, thought Morris.

He told her how he bumped into the astronaut Neil Armstrong whilst testing the new spacesuits.

'Do they get hot inside the suits?' she asked.

'Oh yes, so I worked with a scientist to create a cold airflow, it's called "thermal surface neutralisation".' *Boy, I'm on fire!* 'And, of course, this is the forerunner of thermal underwear coming onto the market soon in this country.' Morris had recently seen a Damart thermal underwear brochure at the doctor's surgery.

She smiled, not sure whether he was joking, but felt comfortable with him as their journey progressed. The miles went alarmingly fast as the Rover reached fifty-five mph on the straight sections of road.

'Welcome to Telford. Home of the Ironbridge' said the sign.

Morris thought of the small village where he lived just outside Reading. *Welcome to Pangbourne – home of the Bridges. Clever,* he thought.

Ahead was a sign indicating the hospital in one mile. Morris felt a pang of sadness as he was about to lose his lovely young companion, with whom he was able to escape into a fantasy world, the likes of which he had never experienced before.

The wrought iron gates to the hospital entrance came into view. Morris slowly drove into the car park.

She sat there and asked what he was doing in Telford, hoping he had not gone out of his way for her.

'No, no, no,' said Morris. 'I'm meeting a government minister to look at thermal underwear for the armed forces, which will be tested in the Welsh mountains.'

'Here is my number at the nurses' accommodation. If you're in the area again, give me a call. We could have a drink, and I could pay you back for your kindness.'

'Yes. I will. By the way, what's your name?'

'Sarah. Sarah David.'

'My name is Mor.... Mark Leyland,' he replied, seeing a sign for Leyland Motors on the wall opposite.

'OK, thanks again.'

Chapter 3

Morris went into Telford and parked in a municipal car park. He picked up his sample bag and walked into the high street. Woolworths, Burtons, Freeman Hardy Willis, Co-op – it could be anywhere, and then, occupying a large corner plot, Ashford's General Retailers came into view.

Morris entered the shop and saw that ladies' wear was on the second floor, so he took the lift and the whole scene opened up before him. Gent's clothing, children's clothing and ladies' clothing. He went to a highly polished oak counter and was confronted by a lady wearing thick black-framed spectacles with her hair in a bun.

'Good morning. I have an appointment with Miss Jarvis, Head Buyer. I have some new "heads" to show her.' Not a titter, but Morris thought it was amusing.

The lady disappeared behind some curtains before returning. 'Miss Jarvis will see you now, Mr…'

'Leyland,' said Morris, without thinking.

Morris went into an office with a glass panel door. A woman the size of a tank sat behind a leather-topped desk in a tweed suit. Morris gave her his card.

'Ah, Mr Bridges…' she said, hesitating. 'I thought my assistant said your name was Leyland?'

'Oh, how strange,' said Morris.

'What can I do for you?' said The Tank.

'Well, my company specialises in undergarments for the discerning lady. Ladies who know their own mind and want support where support is most wanted.' Morris, realising Miss

Jarvis was indeed the likely target wearer of triple XL knickers, thought if he made her think she was the norm he should get an order easily. 'The trend nowadays is to make underwear far too skinny, which may suit the youngsters, but women like yourself want stability, firmness and knowing that the elastic waistband won't lose its grip. Good British know-how,' he continued.

'It says on the label "Made in Malta",' said Miss Jarvis.

'Ah yes, but with British cotton, which is more durable than other makes.'

The rise of chain stores such as Marks and Spencer's and Littlewoods meant that independent department stores were struggling to hold their customer base. But, said Morris, 'This was a chance to bring back your typical British housewife who appreciates the comfort of triple XL Holdall Knickers.'

'Makes sense,' said Miss Jarvis. 'I'll take a hundred pairs, various sizes, and I trust you will leave a sample?'

'No problem,' he said. 'I will find a pair of medium size as you are a little slimmer than our target market,' he lied.

When he got back to the car he cut off the triple XL label, wrapped them in tissue and returned to the store with the gift for Miss Jarvis.

The Tank was now walking around the second floor with new purpose, but finding it hard to hold in her waistline much longer.

Morris returned to his car, having bought a pork pie and fizzy drink, and sat thinking of his next call in Chester that afternoon. But he didn't want to leave Telford – not many people have said that.

Just up the road was a pretty nurse who seemed to enjoy his lifestyle and exciting things he did for a living. Morris dreamt of sitting at the wheel of a Jaguar with personal number plates ML 100 as he headed north to Chester. Sitting next to him was this pretty young thing in a nurse's outfit. They will be staying in the best upmarket hotel in Cheshire, whereby the valet would take his car and park it up with a name tag marked Mark Leyland on the ignition keys. They would have champagne delivered to the room, and then she would slowly—

Bugger, he thought as the Rover came to grinding halt due to a puncture.

Morris pulled over into a field entrance and wondered where the handbook might be. Eventually he found it and proceeded to change the tyre. This was going to make him late for his next appointment in Chester. *I must find a phone box in the next village.*

'Hello, is that Jones and Jones of Chester?'

'Yes it is.'

'Good, could you tell your buyer, Mr Peabody, I've had a mechanical problem and won't make it until tomorrow afternoon? Thank you.'

'Who shall I say called?'

'Mor... Mark Leyland.'

It was late afternoon and Morris found himself thinking about Telford again, which is unhealthy for any man. He bought some food and a newspaper in a village shop before returning to his car, but he decided to sit in a park just off the village centre.

Children were playing on the swings and young mothers were chatting about motherhood as if they had just discovered it, not realising that babies have been around for centuries. Morris thought, *wait till they have a 'Stanley', that will shut them up.*

Morris thought he had better phone Penelope and explain he won't be home tonight because of the puncture and he still had some calls to make tomorrow.

Penelope took it in her stride and whilst trying to take a bite from a Mars bar dropped the phone, leaving Morris hanging there. 'Sorry,' she said.

'Bye.'

Morris noticed a small branch of Lloyds Bank in the village centre and decided he needed some money out of his account. Lots of it. Well, £20.

He pushed the cheque for £20 cash across the counter.

The cashier looked at him with a stern furrowing of the brow. 'Do you have any identification, sir?' said Stern Face.

'Oh yes, here's my driving licence.'

The transaction complete, Morris walked out of the bank and returned to the Rover. It was now late afternoon in August. The time was four o'clock and he decided to make the most daring decision of his entire life. Phone Sarah – Telford 54369.

Eventually someone picked up the phone.

'Hello, can I speak to Sarah?'

'She's not back yet.'

'When do you think she will be back?'

'Difficult, she's gone food shopping.'

'Who's calling?'

'Mark Leyland.'

'Try later.'

Morris sadly put the phone down and pondered his next move. He thought if he went at fifty mph he could buy some clothes that befit a man who meets ministers and travels to America. He rushed back to Telford and parked behind '50 Shilling Tailor' just before the store was about to close.

'We are about to close the shop, sir.'

'It's all right. I know exactly what I want. A pair of trousers and a coloured shirt,' said Morris. He had never bought a coloured shirt before. He tried them on. Perfect.

He came out of the shop, crossed the road and walked through an alley leading to the car park. As he rounded the corner, *bump, crash* and an explosion of groceries went all over the pavement.

'I'm so sorry,' said Morris not looking up. 'Let me help you.' They both grappled with the shopping.

'Why, Mark. What are you doing here?' said Sarah.

'Pardon?'

'Mark, you gave me a lift today. It's me, Sarah.'

'Good gracious. Here let me help you,' said Morris somewhat confused. *Is this destiny?*

'What are you doing back in Telford? I thought you were going to the Welsh mountains with the British army chiefs.'

'It was raining,' said Morris, quickly.

'I thought your specialist clothing could resist anything, especially a downpour,' said Sarah slightly mocking.

Morris thought, *that's right, especially the double gusset version!*

'I needed some food as I've just moved into new lodgings and the cupboard is bare.'

Morris tried to avoid the connotation between Sarah and 'bare'. He looked across the road and noticed a Lyons tea shop.

'Could I buy you a cup of tea and Chelsea bun to make up for my causing you to drop your groceries?'

'Well, I was going home to cook myself an omelette. But why not?'

The streets were practically empty. The shops were closing and the workers were cashing up their tills after another boring day. As they entered the tea shop, the bell on the door made a resounding clang. Instinctively everybody looked up. Morris thought, *yeah, she's with me – so what?*

A plastic top table was being cleared, so they made their way to sit down.

Morris was now carrying Sarah's shopping and felt something wet and soggy just where his hand was holding the bag. *Probably the eggs,* he thought. *Better not say anything.*

'Can I help you?'

'Tea for two and Chelsea buns, please.'

'What about your daughter?' said the waitress in a matter-of-fact sort of way.

'She's not my daught— Oh, forget it, just bring tea for two and two buns.'

'We're closing in twenty minutes.'

'Well, you'd better hurry up, then,' said Morris, feeling assertive. 'Typical British attitude,' Morris said to Sarah.

'Perhaps she's got a problem – children or husband, who knows,' said Sarah. 'Are you married?' she continued.

'No,' said Morris, 'a widower.'

'Oh, I'm so sorry.'

'It's water under the bridge now. *Or Bridges*, mused Morris, excusing the pun.

'Was she ill?' said Sarah.

'No, no. She fell off an elephant in India,' said Morris.

'Gracious, how tragic.'

'Yes, a dog barked at the great mammoth and it reared up – she fell crashing onto the ground on her head.'

'Were you on holiday?'

'No, I was on business negotiating a new railroad system.'

Sarah supped at her tea and slowly nibbled at her bun.

Morris was still getting over the shock of having told a lie again, but it was so easy – and he liked it!

'Where do you live?' said Sarah.

Pangbourne in Berkshire sounded rather dull for a man of the world, so seeing the bun in front of him he answered, 'Oh, Chelsea.'

'That's posh, do you see any celebrities?'

'One is always bumping into the odd star. Michael Caine and I go running in Hyde Park together most weekends. Nice guy – not many people know that.'

God, that was rather obvious, thought Morris. He suddenly pulled in his midriff to obscure the fact that running was the last thing he would consider doing.

'Sometimes, weather permitting, I have a game of golf at Wentworth with Bruce Forsyth and Henry Cooper, but my handicap needs improving.'

'Oh,' said Sarah, 'I hadn't noticed you were handicapped. What is it?'

'No, my handicap is ten,' said Morris.

'Never heard of that in the nursing profession,' said Sarah.

Morris realised the conversation had gone awry and looked for a diversion. On the cream glossed walls were posters of musical shows and plays at the Telford Playhouse. He noticed that tonight was a special one-off performance of *The Mousetrap* by the Shropshire Amateur Dramatic Society, or S.A.D.S. Morris decided to change the subject.

'Do you like the theatre or movies?'

'Yes,' said Sarah, 'but living on a nurse's wage doesn't allow anything left over for frivolities.'

Morris thought this was a once in a lifetime opportunity to be bold and with some trepidation asked the question, 'Would you like to go to the theatre tonight?' Knowing from the moist patch in the grocery bag, omelette was probably off the evening menu.

'Don't you have to go back home?'

'Not really as we're trying the thermal underwear neutralisation test again tomorrow, so I've decided to stay in Telford.'

'Where are you staying?'

'Oh-oh, Lipton Towers,' he answered quickly espying an advert for Lipton's Tea, 'it's government owned.'

'OK,' said Sarah, 'would love to. What time?'

Blimey, thought Morris, *this is getting out of control – wonderfully so.* 'Seven o'clock at your flat?' he said.

They finished their tea and gathered up the groceries. Morris suggested he drop her off at the nurse lodgings, which she gratefully accepted.

'See you later,' she said, smiling. As she walked towards the communal door, the bottom of her shopping bag fell through releasing all its contents on the doorstep.

Morris pretended not to notice and sped away to 'Lipton Towers'.

Chapter 4

Morris had always kept very tight purse strings on the Bridges' finances, with Penelope knowing nothing that went on. She was content as long as she could sit and read soppy novels, watch TV, and there was always a plentiful supply of chocolate.

Buying a new anything would take Morris days to work out the best deal and then he would endeavour to get a discount, as buyers were always attempting to obtain one from him, even in ladies' underwear.

So sitting in the car working out what the evening might cost, he decided to seek out the cheapest bed and breakfast establishment in Telford. He bought the local rag and looked up classifieds under the heading 'B & B'.

10 SHILLINGS PER NIGHT – NO TOWELS OR PRO'S.

Towel he had. Pro – definitely not! He found a phone box and called the number.

'Yes,' said a gruff voice.

'Do you have any vacancies?'

'Yep, a single and no women, understand – the police already think I run a brothel – bloody cheek. I run a clean house here, you understand?'

'OK,' said Morris, somewhat alarmed.

He followed the directions down the back streets of Telford and row after row of terraced back-to-back houses until he saw The Black Pig public house on the corner. This was his accommodation for the night. He parked in the yard, went through the back door and approached the bar.

'Hello!' said Morris. 'Hello.'

'I heard you the first time,' came a voice, followed by a caricature of an ex-wrestler with cauliflower ears, broken nose and a dirty vest. 'You phoned just now? Ten shillings, please.'

No 'welcome to our humble abode', thought Morris. He took out his wallet exposing the £20 he'd recently withdrawn from the bank.

The innkeeper noticing the wad licked his lips. 'You can't be too careful round here, so if you would like to leave your valuables and wallet in the secure safe overnight, you can sleep easy, if you know what I mean.' As Morris didn't take him up on his offer, he continued, 'This way.' They made their way up two flights of stairs and along a poorly lit corridor with a single bulb hanging precariously from the ceiling.

'Room four, overlooking the gardens. I lock up at eleven, so if you're too late you'll have to stay out.' He then slammed the door and left.

Morris looked around the room. *Bloody hell,* he thought, *for a man who runs with Michael Caine this is a bit of a comedown.* A stained top bedcover, a sideboard with a drawer missing, a cracked mirror and a cupboard – no, wrong – bathroom, which hadn't seen any Flash for some time.

Oh well, better than nothing, he thought. *No, it wasn't,* he thought again. *Nothing didn't have stains, nothing didn't smell, nothing was infinitely better.*

Morris suddenly looked at his watch. *Hell, six forty-five already.* He quickly changed into his nice new clothes. *Is the pink shirt a bit too – you know – poncey? No, go for it,* he decided.

As he left the back door, a group of youths had gathered around the Rover 75 with the look of 'how can we inflict damage on a rich git who parked in our territory'.

'Hey, get away,' said Morris.

The group formed a phalanx behind one particularly gruesome looking youth.

'What ya doing here?' said the moron.

'I'm a football scout for Arsenal looking for local talent. Tell me, young man, where's the local park so I can see if there are any future stars in Telford?'

'I can play a bit,' said a second youth.

'And me,' said a third.

Morris looked them up and down and said, 'OK, I'll give you a chance. Meet me in the park at seven thirty with your boots.'

Morris jumped into the Rover and burnt rubber getting away. Well, perhaps a yard of gravel, and headed towards the nurses' lodgings ten minutes away.

Should one park outside or a little up the road? What was the norm in these circumstances? How would he know?

He parked up the road just in case somebody from Pangbourne –150 miles away – should be walking down the street by the nursing accommodation in Telford. *Unlikely, but you never know. You can't be too careful,* thought Morris.

His natural juices were becoming apparent, but not in the right place. He angled his rear view mirror to inspect under his arms to see damp patches appearing. *What to do?* He decided to walk up and down the road with his arms outstretched and waving as if to take off. He hoped this would overcome the slight embarrassment on his important mission to impress a pretty young thing.

Unfortunately Morris didn't notice the blue Ford Anglia with a black and white chequered pattern on the side and 'POLICE' written quite clearly on the front and rear. As the car drew alongside, the passenger window was wound down.

'Evening, sir,' came the quizzical Shropshire accent. 'You will never get off the ground unless you run faster.'

'Thank you, Officer,' said Morris, 'I'll try that.'

'Nutter,' the police officer said to his driver. 'Let's leave him be as we should've been off duty ten minutes ago and the paperwork's not worth it. After all, imitating a bird is not a crime – look at Rod Hull and Emu.'

Morris's waving of arms was suddenly halted when he noticed Sarah coming towards him.

'What did they want?' she asked.

'They recognised me and wanted to know if I wanted police protection whilst in Telford. I explained I was incognito so best left alone,' said Morris. 'Let's go.'

Off the Rover went towards the Telford Playhouse in the town centre. Morris parked near the theatre and escorted Sarah up the stone steps and into the shabby foyer where two old ladies were excitingly buying tickets.

'Do you have two tickets for tonight's performance, please?'

'Front, middle or back?'

'Back, please.'

'That'll be half a crown.'

Morris and Sarah entered the auditorium and in the half-light could see the great threadbare red curtains with 'Safety Curtain' handwritten on a piece of cardboard.

A torch appeared with an elderly lady behind it. *Very similar looking to the lady selling tickets,* Morris thought.

'What numbers?'

'J twenty-two and twenty-three,' said Morris.

'Down there on the right.'

'Thank you,' said Morris. 'Don't wear your torch out, will you?'

They sat down and commented that there seemed to be a lot of empty seats. In fact, apart from the two old ladies, there was no one else.

The lights dimmed and the curtains opened showing a roomful of brown furniture and backdrops painted by the local painter and decorator with a lot of grey paint left over from a previous job, possibly a battleship.

The actors started to speak, oblivious to the empty auditorium, and then the star made an entrance falling over a stool, obviously worse for drink. He gathered his composure and looked out into the theatre. After seeing it was empty, he looked at Morris and Sarah and in a slurred voice said, 'Have you not got something better to do than watch dried up old has-beens whose last-ditch attempt to be spotted by an impresario is just a load of old bollocks?' He then proceeded to fall over again, pulling the safety curtain on top of him.

Morris hadn't been to the theatre for many years and assumed it to be a bit more professional here in the sixties and swinging England – this was not what he expected.

Fearful that they may be called upon to take part in audience participation, Morris and Sarah quietly left.

'Good old Dalton Rigby. A very fine actor and, between you and me, Sarah, a very good agent during the war. He foiled a plot to kill Churchill and the Nazis are still hunting for him, so he uses the stage and several pseudonyms to keep on the move and keep them guessing.'

'Really,' said Sarah. 'What should we do now, then? How about a meal? I couldn't do an omelette, all the eggs were broken.'

You can't make an omelette without breaking eggs, thought Morris.

Chapter 5

Morris, not knowing the area, had no idea where to go.

'I know a little place down on the river. Let's go there,' said Sarah.

Sounds expensive, thought Morris. But he couldn't cry wolf now; he was in it up to his neck.

'Lovely,' said Morris.

They travelled five miles down a winding road and came to the Riverboat Inn. There were tables on the grassy banks of the river with candles in glasses and serviettes. There was also a pianist playing romantic songs for swinging lovers. *Everything that made it look expensive,* thought Morris.

They were escorted to a table near the river. The warm evening air created a feeling, for Morris, of magic.

'Would madam and sir like to see the wine list? We have a delightful Chardonnay just in and we're the only restaurant in Shropshire permitted to sell it, it is so special, madam?'

'I do like a taste of wine. How about you, Mark? You must be an expert with all your travelling and high-class friends?' said Sarah.

'Yes, of course, we must try a little,' Morris said, hoping they took cheques.

The appetisers were a delightful mixture of seafood and the main meal an exquisite choice of fish or lamb.

Morris instinctively chose the cheapest option, whereas Sarah had acquired the taste of the rich life very quickly, or her background was a little more upper class than she let on.

The pianist continued playing music for the right mood – Sinatra, Dean Martin, Al Martino – and the wine was beginning to make Sarah's head a little light. When she saw the musician get up to take a break, she said to Morris, confidently, 'Watch this.'

She leapt from her chair and made towards the piano. Morris froze with trepidation and noticed everyone was looking at him.

Sarah sat at the piano, flexed her fingers and went into a faultless rendition of Rachmaninov. As she played, her shoulders and neck created the shape of someone in touch with her artistry and her fingers floated feather-like across the keys.

Morris sat open-mouthed in admiration of this beautiful girl who he was accompanying for the evening. *Am I dreaming? Was this real? Haven't phoned Penelope. Oh, sod it!*

Sarah finished, stood up and acknowledged the warm applause, including the refreshed pianist, and sat back down with Morris.

Actually sit with Morris, me, he thought, *an underwear salesman – sorry, a friend of Michael Caine.* 'Why are you studying to be a nurse when you can play like that? You could be a star!'

'Oh, it's nothing. As I said, my father was a conductor and my mother taught piano, but I felt I wanted to contribute more to life and help others.'

'But nursing pays peanuts and pianists are…well, rich,' said Morris.

'Well, it goes back a bit deeper than that. As I said my father is a conductor, but he was born Joseph Davidovic in Russia and defected to the west a few years ago. The Russians didn't approve that such a high profile musician should reject their way of life for the tawdriness of the west. I was a little girl then and didn't understand, but we seemed to be on the move all the time until we came to England and felt safe. Father continues to compose and conduct and makes a good living whilst Mother teaches piano.'

Morris was beginning to wonder if he was in a dream and any minute Penelope was going to advise him his bowls shirt was washed and ironed.

As they got up to leave, the other customers began to applaud and Morris heard them say, 'Thank you!' and 'Safe journey!' and then, 'Lucky man!' *Lucky man, indeed.*

Morris opened the passenger door of the Rover and made a gallant swoop with his arm. 'Madam, your carriage awaits.'

They pulled out of the car park and back along the winding road with the headlights picking out the green overhanging hedgerows like an eternal tunnel of green.

Morris noticed headlights in his rearview mirror that seemed unnecessarily close. *Perhaps it was someone in the restaurant wanting Sarah's autograph.*

They entered the outskirts of Telford, and Morris was wondering how the night should end. He wasn't a promiscuous man and sex was not a high priority in his life. He would just drop her off, a quick peck on the cheek and avoid The Black Pig, having paid his ten shillings – he didn't turn up for football training so felt it prudent not to return to the area.

The nurses' accommodation loomed ahead. Morris stopped the car, turned to Sarah and smiled.

'That was the loveliest night of my life and I owe it all to you for being such surprising company,' he said.

'Mark, I enjoyed it, too. It's nice to meet a successful, older man who is just unassuming and gentle and I somehow feel safe with him. That hasn't always been the case.'

Mark winced a little at being 'older' and 'safe': a double whammy.

'When your work with the government brings you back this way, we shall do it again. Promise me, Mark,' said Sarah.

She leant over and gave Morris a kiss on the cheek. 'Bye, Mark.'
'Pardon?'
'Bye,' she repeated.
'Oh yes, I shall call you.'

Chapter 6

She opened the door, slid out of the seat and walked the fifty yards to the entrance of her accommodation.

Then all hell broke out.

Two men in dark raincoats ran up behind Sarah and bundled her into a black Mercedes.

The lights in the rearview mirror, Morris recalled. He sat there transfixed. *What the hell is happening?*

The Mercedes raced off. Morris instinctively went after them. When they realised he was following, the streets of Telford became Brooklands racing circuit. Now Morris had never driven the Rover with any purpose, it was never necessary before, but now the one bright spot in his life was being kidnapped. *Why?*

The big Merc wallowed from side to side on the corners, and the passengers were visibly being thrown around, but the Rover was steady and kept on their tail. As they left Telford and headed for open countryside the speed increased to over seventy mph.

'Christ,' said Morris, holding his buttocks to prevent any slippage, in any form.

The country roads were full of bends and bumps, and Morris was gradually losing them as the Merc's more powerful motor pulled away.

He had lost them now and was at his wits' end sat at a crossroads.

Which way? Why Sarah? Must phone Penelope. Concentrate, man. Concentrate.

As he looked both ways with his window down, he heard the distant screeching of brakes. He immediately made off in that direction. *What if they've had an accident? What about poor Sarah?*

He approached a humpback bridge and when halfway over he was confronted with a scene of carnage. The Mercedes was upside down and a cow stood in the middle of the road. Two dark figures were crawling around in the road somewhat dazed. *Where's Sarah?*

He stopped the Rover, ran up to the scene and searched. She was nowhere to be seen. He went to the upturned car; there was petrol everywhere.

It might blow up. No time for cowardice, Morris thought. *I must find her.*

As he looked in the Merc he could see a slumped female form in the back seat, upside down, groaning, but alive.

He hadn't taken much notice of first-aid training in the Scouts but was a first-aider with the Berkshire Spire group, although never called upon – apart from when the chairman sat on a wasp on a gravestone and ran around the churchyard with his trousers down, which inspired the local newspaper headline 'Chairman inSPIRED in Bum Deal at Gravestone'.

'Sarah, speak to me,' said Morris.

More groans, but slowly he put his arm around her, easing her the right way up, and lifted her to the ground.

'Are you all right?'

'I think so, apart from my head,' she said.

Morris then realised she had ripped her dress and was revealing more than was decent. Her soft, silky breasts were exposed; fortunately, for his eyes only. *Concentrate, Morris.*

The two dark figures were coming to their senses, and then Morris noticed something that horrified him. One of them, with his back to Morris, had a gun.

Morris, not usually given to swearing, said, 'Shit,' and grabbed a piece of wood. With all his might he delivered a mighty blow to the back of the gunman's head. Unfortunately this caused the gun to go off and shoot the cow, who was licking the other figure, number two, on the face. The cow collapsed on the poor fellow pushing out any air he had in his lungs.

Morris was confronted with a squashed kidnapper, a dead cow, a second kidnapper with a crushed skull and a pretty young girl with a silky white breast exposed. *This shouldn't happen to an underwear salesman,* he thought.

He went back to Sarah, covered her modesty with a blanket and put his arm around her.

'Oh, Mark, I'm so sorry to get you involved in all this, but you were magnificent, my hero,' said Sarah.

Morris then saw headlights slowly approaching and realised it was a tractor. Whoever it was, they were going to be confronted with the scene of two dead men, a dead cow and an upturned Mercedes. *The farmer's going to be upset about the cow,* he thought.

'Quick, get in the Rover, we must go.'

He turned the Rover around and sped along the country roads at speeds he had never experienced before, but he didn't care; he was a murderer, twice over, and an animal slaughterer. *I must phone Penelope,* he thought to himself.

They travelled for miles towards Wales, he guessed, and came to a village where he saw a phone box lit up. It was four minutes past midnight, a bit late for Penelope, but here goes. He told Sarah he had to report in – the usual stuff.

'Hello, Penny, how are you?'

'In bed. Where are you and why are you calling so late?'

'Problem with the car again, love.' *I never call her love.* 'Any phone calls?'

'Yes, just one from the chairman of your spire thing, could you make three o'clock on Saturday as he's heard of an interesting tower with unusual brickwork. It's about twenty-five miles from Reading. I said you'd be interested, just to bring some excitement into your life.'

'I will, dear. Running out of money, speak soon, bye.'

Chapter 7

Morris returned to the car where Sarah was adjusting her dress to cover up her beautiful right breast. Morris assumed the left one was just as beautiful and smashed his head on the door frame getting into the car. *God!*

'What now?' they said in unison.

'Well an explanation would suffice, Sarah. As it stands I've been involved in a double murder, with a cow as the main suspect. I've driven at speeds that James Hunt, the racing driver, would have been proud of, and I've befriended a nurse who turns out to be a maestro of the piano, and all you can say is, "What now!" Let's go shoot a nun or break into Boots and steal drugs! I'm confused, Sarah, these things don't happen to an undergarment salesman.'

'Pardon, Mark?'

'Oh...whatever. Why did those thugs kidnap you? Is there a shortage of nurses wherever they come from?'

'Mark, listen, I told you my father fled Russia, running away from the Soviet regime, well he said some pretty nasty things about the state of Russia when he was in America and the KGB had threatened to get their revenge. They get upset over the silliest things—'

'Silly?'

'Listen, Mark, my father has pretty good security in this country, which, of course, you know about in your job, but they somehow got a letter to him saying they would get his daughter, me, when next performing in concert, so I decided to become a nurse and blend into the background. I'm sorry about the piano playing earlier on, but I couldn't resist the moment as I was enjoying myself so much. The river, the wine – oh, the wine – and the food and most of all you, Mark. I felt free from all the running I've done lately, as though nobody could touch me. But the KGB have been following me for weeks and chose their moment, and now I've involved you.'

'You certainly have,' said Morris.

Morris thought back to that morning. He had completed a deal with Miss Jarvis at Ashford's with some slick salesmanship, paying a good bonus, and life was satisfactory. Tonight he had killed two Russian members of the KGB and a prize cow. How distraught the farmer will be when he finds his cow lying on top of an Eastern European-looking gentleman.

Morris looked through the windscreen of the Rover at nothing. It was pitch black and he was looking towards Wales was all he could ascertain.

Sarah started to cry.

Morris couldn't find his handkerchief, so he grabbed a piece of cloth from the back seat and handed it to her – triple X ladies' knickers, in peach.

Sarah didn't notice at first and blew her nose in the crotch.

Morris winced and tried to grab the knickers back.

'Wait a minute, Mark. What are these? They look like… Oh my God!'

'They have women astronauts as well, you know,' said Morris. 'That is our "Lift-off" range, specially strengthened for the take-off – puts enormous strain on the bowels, you know.'

'Oh, they look very ordinary to me,' said Sarah.

'That's the secret,' said Morris. 'We make everything look standard, but there is very high technology in those knickers.'

Morris was in 'Mark' mode again and forgetting the dilemma he was in: sitting in the Rover 75 with a bedraggled pretty girl, facing Wales, with blood on his hands – possibly the cow's.

Which would confuse the scenes-of-crime team, he thought, *if caught by the police.*

'What do we do now?' asked Sarah.

'Well, if the KGB were on to you, they may know your movements, it would appear, so you can't go back to your place. If there are only two agents in Shropshire, we should be safe.'

'A dozen,' said Sarah. 'There are six hundred agents in the UK alone, all highly trained gunmen. They're everywhere working at bringing down this country. It's rumoured your Prime Minister is one of them,' she said.

'Right,' said Morris, 'only ten to go, then. How many in Wales do you think?'

'Not so many. Who wants Wales anyway? All those sheep and singing miners. Not a great catch, is it?' Sarah said sarcastically.

The moon suddenly appeared from behind a cloud and lit up the front of the car. Morris could see mascara running down Sarah's face making her look like a clown.

'Here, let me wipe your eyes,' he said and proceeded to clean away the black rivulets from her cheeks with the crotch of the triple X knickers.

'They won't explode, will they?' she said, and they both laughed out loud.

Chapter 8

It was two in the morning. They were both now tired. Too late to book a room – sorry, two rooms – and Morris thought it best they parked up for the night in a field and slept.

There was a gap in the hedge just ahead of them, so Morris slowly steered the Rover through the gate and thought it safe to apply the handbrake and settle for the night.

He always kept a blanket in the boot and an overcoat, so he gave her the former and put the seat back as far as possible. He suggested they'll be able to think a little straighter in the morning.

The moon disappeared again behind cloud cover. Morris lay there recording the day he'd had. *Was this all really happening?* He slowly went into a deep sleep.

Suddenly Morris woke with a start and found Sarah shouting, 'Albert, Albert!'

'Who? What? Where?' cried Morris.

'My budgie, Albert. I've forgotten about him, he's alone in the nurses' accommodation, he'll be hungry.'

Morris had never been a great pet lover and his first instinct was 'so what'.

'Well, tomorrow, we could phone the flats and ask one of the other nurses to feed him.'

'They can't get in,' said Sarah. 'We'll have to go back.'

'Now, wait a minute,' said Morris, somewhat alarmed at the prospect of travelling back, a long way back, to Telford. He had made a mental note never to go back to Telford, and he hoped

Ashford's department store went broke so he would never have to return.

Sarah started to cry again; Morris knew he was on to a loser.

He started the Rover, reversed out of the field and went back the way he had come, hardly keeping his eyes open enough to drive.

Sarah was so grateful. She placed her hand on his on the wheel and gave it a warm squeeze.

'Welcome to Telford. Home of the Ironbridge' said the sign, again.

'Bollocks,' said Morris under his breath.

As they approached the nurses' lodgings, Morris switched off his lights so as not to alert any reinforcement KGB officers hiding in the shadows.

He stopped the car outside. Sarah jumped out, ran to the door and let herself in. She quickly gathered some clothes and, of course, Albert the budgie.

Meanwhile, Morris decided to get out of the car thinking it might help to keep him awake if he did some exercises on the road. Just as he was completing his fourth press-up, he was aware of headlights immediately behind him. *Oh no,* he thought, *this is it. I'm going to die in Telford, shot by the KGB's best agents.*

'Evening, sir,' said the voice. 'Have we crash landed, sir? I told you yesterday evening you would never get off the ground.'

Morris realised it was the same member of the Shropshire Constabulary he encountered yesterday whilst trying to get rid of the damp patches under his armpits.

'Evening, Officer, just looking for my dog under the car.'

'Isn't it time you were locked up, sir, for the night... Sorry, go to bed? It is three thirty in the morning.'

Just then Sarah came running out of the gates loaded with four bags and a budgie.

'What's up, Mark?'

'Sorry, miss, it's time your dear old dad was in bed,' said the officer. 'We found him lying in the road looking for his dog.'

'Dog?' said Sarah. 'Oh yes, sorry, Officer, we're just about to go on holiday. Early morning flight, you know,' said Sarah.

'With a budgie? Can't he fly on his own?' said the officer.

'It's going into a bird sanctuary for lonely birds,' said Morris.

'Why, is he not well? I had a mate once who bred budgies, made a fortune, set up his own "Budgie Airline".'

The connection between budget air flights and budgies was not lost on Morris.

Whilst the two officers fell about laughing, the sound of their laughter was such that a lady at number 74 opened her bedroom window and shouted, 'Do you know what time it is?'

'Yes, ma'am, three thirty-five a.m. precisely,' said the police officer.

'I will call the police,' she barked. To which the two police officers pulled themselves together, climbed into the Panda car and sped off towards the town centre.

Morris and Sarah loaded everything into the Rover and followed signs to anywhere, away from Telford.

Chapter 9

They were the only car on the road for miles and miles. Sarah chatted away non-stop about what a mess they were in and it was all her fault. Will Morris lose his job if they found out he had killed two diplomats (spies) and a cow – unlawful slaughter for all three probably.

Morris didn't need reminding. He could only guess what sort of state he'd be in to see the head buyer of the ladies' section at Jones and Jones of Chester in a few hours. His pinstripe suit and bowler hat were somewhere under Sarah's bags and budgie. He hadn't shaved and his white shirt was no longer hanging serenely on a hanger.

It was nearly 6:30 a.m. and Cheshire was beginning to come to life with milk floats, paperboys and shift workers going about their routines unaware of the black Rover cruising down the road.

'Why are we in Chester when you said you had to meet a government minister and army chiefs in rural Wales, Mark?' she said.

'Well, I thought I would drop you off at the bus station so you could clean up and have breakfast whilst I go to the Welsh mountains, and then you could leave your stuff in the lost property and look around Chester.'

There should be some wash facilities in the bus station, and Morris thought it a good opportunity for them both to get back to some sort of reality.

'Do you want me to leave on a bus to somewhere, Mark, get out of your hair? As I dragged you into my life with dire consequences, but to some extent your life must be quite exciting as well?'

'If only you knew, my dear.'

Was this the time to tell the truth, that he was a traveller selling ladies' underwear to department stores, that he was married and lived in Berkshire, that he had never been to America, or met Michael Caine or Henry Cooper.

The only exciting thing that has happened in the last twenty years was winning the Mixed Pairs Bowling Cup with Wendy Struthers and receiving a trophy and big kiss from his partner, which would have been all right if her wig hadn't got caught in his watch. When they lifted the cup above their heads for a photo in *The Herald* it revealed a different looking Wendy.

Morris got fed up with jokes regarding 'hair-raising cup final' and 'perhaps you should try crown green bowling'.

Probably best they get cleaned up using the municipal bus company's facilities and tell her over breakfast.

Chapter 10

After twenty minutes they emerged looking spick and span with Sarah looking particularly beautiful in a fresh floral dress. Morris had managed to smooth most of the creases out of his pinstripe suit and white shirt.

They sat in the car and Morris, unaccustomed as he was, braced himself to tell Sarah the truth when Albert, the budgie, screeched, 'Give us a kiss!' which threw Morris off his farewell speech.

'Let's eat somewhere,' said Morris.

'Will you have time if you have a long journey to Wales?'

'Oh, they can wait until I arrive.'

'Wow,' said Sarah, 'you must be important.'

'Yes, well, let's talk about it over breakfast, shall we?'

Across the road was a shabby cafe that boasted the 'Best British Fried Breakfast in Chester', so in they went and sat next to the window with the chintz curtains and chintz tablecloth.

'Can I help you?' said the waitress.

'Full English breakfast, please,' said Morris, 'and two cups of tea.'

'Bacon with that?'

'Er, yes please,' said Morris raising his eyebrows to Sarah.

'What about eggs – fried, scrambled or poached?'

'Scrambled.' Again he looked at Sarah and she nodded approval.

'Beans on the fried bread or on the side?'

'Umm…on the side.'

'Sausage – one or two?'

'What's the difference?' said Morris becoming sarcastic. 'You get twice as many with two.'

'Could you possibly hurry up? We're in a rush,' said Morris.

'Are you in a hurry to get away from me, Mark? Is your government business more interesting? I can understand that. I'll finish my breakfast, then catch a bus to Liverpool. I can't go home to Father as they'll be watching for me returning home at some stage. Perhaps I can find a job in Liverpool with my nursing experience, which isn't a great deal, and find some digs for myself and Albert, but my funds are running low, so it won't be much.'

Morris wasn't really listening. He was gazing out of the window nervously trying to put some order into how he was going to tell her the truth.

The waitress placed the two plates in front of them with a thud. 'Do you want sauce? We've got both sorts, red or brown?'

'Whatever,' he answered, now getting exasperated. Morris was about to taste the delights of a burnt sausage when he found himself looking through the window again. He now noticed two dark-clothed gentlemen taking an interest in the Rover across the street. *Are they police? Are there parking restrictions in the street? Surely not...*

'Oh my God,' he said to himself recognising the Russian he hit over the head with a piece of wood. *How the hell did they find us here? Sarah did say they were everywhere, but Chester?* Morris wondered what to do. *Cause a diversion,* he thought.

The proprietor of the cafe was standing behind a counter with a limp cigarette hanging from his mouth.

Morris walked towards him with his full English breakfast and shouted, 'This food is disgusting. I wouldn't feed it to a pig!' and proceeded to pour the contents down the rather large owner's front.

The other customers looked on in astonishment, as did Sarah. *What's he doing?* she thought. *He's flipped!*

As soon as the egg and beans started to run down the cafe proprietor's grubby apron, a red mist descended over his eyes. He grabbed a very long knife and shouted, 'You will pay for this!'

The cafe door was open, and when the two KGB men heard the commotion they walked briskly to their car fifty yards up the street.

Morris quickly grabbed Sarah and ran to the Rover, jumped in and put the key in the ignition.

Nothing happened.

'Not now, you bitch!' shouted Morris with Sarah looking bemused by the whole thing.

He turned it again and the engine burst into life.

The cafe man was halfway across the street waving a long knife in one hand and a meat cleaver in the other.

Morris put his foot down, almost running over the mad cafe owner who threw his cleaver at the passing car, which flew through the back window and unfortunately the bamboo cage that was Albert's home. The bird fell off his perch.

'Shit, he's killed Albert! What's going on, Mark? Why did you do that?'

'Look out the back!'

Sarah turned around and saw a black Mercedes following at speed.

They raced along streets full of people going to work and children on their way to school, many having to leap out of the way, as a scene from a Hollywood movie unfolded before their eyes.

Morris was involved in a high-speed car chase with not only the KGB, but now the local constabulary had decided to join in and follow him.

Morris saw the sign for North Wales A55. He decided to follow that route, as did the black Mercedes and police car with sirens blaring.

Never had Morris been in trouble with the police before, let alone the KGB, and breaking the law was not his style. But this was an emergency – there was a young girl in need of help.

Beads of sweat ran down his nose as he gripped the wheel until his knuckles were white.

'Go faster, Mark!' shouted Sarah.

'I'm not Mark, I'm Morris!'

'What?'

'My name is Morris Bridges, not Mark Leyland,' he said, realising the truth might as well come out now; he was going to die anyway.

'Why, is that your pseudonym in the government?'

'I don't work for the government. Not now, or ever.'

The houses flashed by and they were now hitting the countryside.

'They're catching us up, Mark...Morris...whatever your name is.'

Morris thought it better to go on country roads so they wouldn't have the chance to pass. He suddenly veered off the main thoroughfare and took a narrow road in the general direction of what he thought was Wales.

The menacing Merc managed to turn off behind Morris, but the police car reacted too late; they tried to negotiate an oak tree but failed in a pile of steam and bent metal.

'Then, who the hell are you and why are you running from the KGB and police?' asked Sarah.

The Rover approached a humpback bridge and nearly left the ground, but not quite, Morris thinking that the springs might not be up to it.

The Merc took it at full speed and landed almost on the back of the Rover. As it hit the road with a thump, two of the tyres burst and the Merc became uncontrollable. It made a hole straight through a hedge with a resounding thud.

Morris pulled in at the side of the road to listen for any signs of life. He gingerly walked back to the gap in the hedge. There was the Merc in a cloud of steam and smoke impaled into a horse, which was astride the bonnet with its head through the windscreen facing two dazed men in black.

Morris ran back to the Rover, jumped in and sped off down the lane.

'What happened?' asked Sarah.

'Oh, the Merc has just gained some more horsepower under the bonnet – or over it,' said Morris.

Chapter 11

Morris gave a great sigh of relief and drove nervously onward.

'You were saying, Morris, that you didn't work for the government and Mark's not your real name. Tell me more. I thought I knew you, but obviously I don't.'

Morris pulled into a layby and stopped the engine.

'What should we do about Albert?' said Morris sadly.

'Well, he's no bloody good now, is he?' said Sarah.

Morris thought, *he wasn't much bloody good before!* Morris had never been a pet lover. They made demands on you and took a lot of time, then you grow to love them, and then they die leaving you sad.

Penelope wanted a Jack Russell once, Morris recalled, and they had one on trial for a week, but the kennel owners took it back after Stanley mixed cannabis with his Pal dog food. The dog climbed the tree and wouldn't come down until the fireman, who Penelope had summoned, called the dog. It leapt thirty feet straight into the fishpond thinking it was a big dog food dish. The vet said it was a miracle it didn't drown, but it should get by on three legs.

'Shall I bury him?' asked Morris.

'No, give him here.' Sarah took hold of the budgie softly, wound down the window and threw it over the hedge saying, 'Oh well.'

Morris sat open-mouthed at the way she had dealt with Albert.

'Where do we go from here?' she asked.

'Well... I have an appointment at Jones and Jones, Outfitters to Gentlefolk, so I may as well keep the appointment and then go back to Chel— Reading.'

'So you really are a travelling salesman for ladies' underwear? All those lies Ma— Morris, and I suppose you're married as well?'

'Well, actually, I'm not,' said Morris, hanging onto the one last bit of the lie that gave him some credibility. 'And how about you? I give you a lift and you tell me you're starting on a nurse's course in Telford, when really you're running away from some of most vicious thugs in the world and you're connected to the whole world of the Cold War, Russia, KGB, nuclear weapons whatever.'

'I wouldn't go quite that far, but you're in it as much as me now – having killed one KGB agent, attacked another one and written off two of their cars, Mark, sorry, Morris.'

Morris thought for a few moments concentrating on road signs to take him to North Wales – why, he had no idea, but he was a wanted man by the most notorious espionage agents in the world. *Oh, to be back looking at church spires,* he contemplated.

'We are on the run,' said Morris in a matter-of-fact sort of way. 'Two desperate souls being chased by assassins, and probably the British police as well.'

'Morris, I'm sorry for the mess we're in. Find a station and I can get a train to somewhere, and you can keep your appointment with Jones and Jones and go back to normal life.'

'Normal life – yes, it was normal, too normal. In the last forty-eight hours I've picked up a stranger, been involved in killing a man from another country, and a cow, had high-speed car chases, walked out of a theatre, eaten divine food and drank divine wine – expensive but lovely – and thrown a full English breakfast at an irate cafe owner. But most of all I've met the loveliest pianist in the whole wide world – and you know what, I don't regret any of it.'

Sarah looked at him, leant over the centre console and kissed him on the cheek. 'You're not so bad yourself when you consider you did all that for me. I will miss you, thank you.'

Morris smiled, checked the rearview mirror and put his foot down, picking up the A55 North Wales coast road.

Chapter 12

Morris looked for a phone box. It was time he reported into his boss at headquarters in Harrogate.

'Hello, Nancy, it's Morris Bridges… Oh, I'm fine, not much happening. Could you put me through to Mr Squires? Thank you.'

'Morris, my boy. How are you? Any orders?'

Mr Squires was third-generation family owners of Squires 'Clothing for the Discerning Lady', but unfortunately cheap imports and the growth of chain stores such as Marks and Spencer's, Littlewoods, etc. had forced Squires to cut down their range to the basics.

'Underwear – you can't beat English cotton next to the skin,' the current Mr Squire's father used to say.

Sadly, the business was declining and Squires specialised in a product line that mostly fashion had walked away from: the larger woman. Twiggy and miniskirts sounded the death knell for larger ladies; they were yesterday, fashion had decreed.

'There's an order in the post for a hundred pairs of Holdall Knickers for Ashford's of Telford. Tough sale, but I broke her down and she gave me the order.'

'Nice going, old chap. Where to next? I believe Jones and Jones were on your itinerary?'

'Oh yes, sad about Jones and Jones, they burnt down last night,' Morris lied.

'Oh dear, missed that on the news,' said Mr Squires. 'Where do you propose going next, Morris? Things are a bit slow here. May have to lay off some girls to tell you the truth. Norman, who covers the north-east, has had a traumatic time lately what with his mother-in-law falling out of her wheelchair and his dog getting run over.'

'Sounds awful,' said Morris. *I wonder how Norman would cope with an irate farmer, a furious cafe owner, two wrecked Mercs and killing a KGB agent?*

'I thought I would try new ground,' said Morris. 'How does southern Ireland sound to you? There's some big lasses there, I hear.' He hadn't, but under the circumstances he thought the Republic of Ireland was well away from twenty KGB agents.

'Great idea! Keep your costs down – hotel, petrol and women,' said Mr Squires with a chuckle.

'If only,' retorted Morris.

'Good luck. Bye.'

Morris returned to the car where Sarah sat looking melancholy.

'I thought you were going to Jones and Jones in Chester, but this road leads to Anglesey?' she said.

'I've decided to try new ground in Ireland, and I would like you to come with me for your own safety.'

'Oh, Morris, how exciting! Thank you. Goodbye Wales, Ireland here we come!'

This is like Bonnie and Clyde, thought Morris. He needed some more money and stopped at a country branch of a bank to withdraw £25. *Hell,* he thought, *if only Penelope could see their statement at the end of the month.*

They approached the ferry at Holyhead, paid the fare and drove aboard, squashed between trucks taking goods to Ireland. Morris decided to take a stroll around the deck of the ferry and leant against the rail as the mainland disappeared over the grey horizon.

What am I doing? he thought to himself. *Running away from what? Some unpleasant things,* he reminded himself and because deep down he felt a sort of parental responsibility towards Sarah. But he soon corrected his thoughts, for this was not a parental thing, it was a feeling of not being able to leave her to fend on her own against this brutal world and feelings were stirring that he had never felt before. He supposed he must have loved Penelope once, but he can't remember when and how.

He remembered how they met at a dance in the local village hall. He could do a quickstep to anything and saw she was left by her friends at a table. Morris approached her tentatively and asked would she like to dance, to which she excitedly jumped up, spilling her Tizer drink down the front of his trousers.

Instead of dancing they rushed to the kitchen where she proceeded to rub down his trousers with a tea towel, oblivious to the personal nature of her movements. Morris stood there saying it was all right, and it was; it was as near to sex that he had ever experienced with a member of the female gender.

Penelope saw his trousers bulge and eased off the wiping down. 'Oh my God!' she cried. This was her first encounter with the male gender, and the reaction to constant rubbing.

Morris said he should go and left, running all the way home.

When he next ventured to the dance hall, a month later, he saw Penelope all alone. He went over and said hello. She lowered her head as if not to hear.

'Would you like to dance?'

Penelope looked around realising it was the only offer she was going to get. She sheepishly stood up, holding her drink firmly, and Morris led her to the floor.

He did the quickstep; she did the waltz – truly a spectacle to behold.

At the end they sat down together and, following some awkward silences, Morris explained he was waiting to join the forces following extensive suitability tests that he'd come through with flying colours. Morris thought this would sound more impressive than the truth, which was serving behind the bacon counter at the Co-op.

Morris rode a bike in those days, which he told Penelope was part of training for quick-response troops in the army. Morris took Penelope home and after three months, as she had intimate knowledge of his private parts, admittedly through grey gabardine trousers, they were engaged to be married. A year later she became Mrs Bridges.

Morris had progressed to become Southern Area Sales Executive for Squires, bought a house for £1200 and life basically became a pattern until Stanley came along and buggered everything up.

Morris had doubts he was the father, but he was comforted in the thought that no one else would voluntarily have intercourse with Penelope. He concluded it must have been after Uncle Jeremiah's funeral when Morris overindulged and had little recollection of the following events, apart from going home in a taxi as he was too intoxicated to drive. Penelope must have seized the moment and got Morris to impregnate her, of which he was completely unaware until Penelope began to put on weight. She often reminded him of their night of passion. As is the British trait, he had sex and didn't even know about it due to the demon drink.

Morris came back to the present when Sarah joined him on deck. She put her arm through his and gave him a smile.

'It's exciting, isn't it?' she said. 'Here we are having only known each other for two days and were running away together. But what do we do when we get to Ireland? Do you have a plan?'

'I suggest we travel from Dublin down the coast to Cork and, assuming we're not being followed at that moment, stay there and collect our thoughts. For now we have three hours to enjoy the boat trip and consider our next move.'

Chapter 13

Morris realised he had never felt like this before. He was on an adventure with a beautiful young girl of Russian descent, at an age when most men are looking forward to their pension, gardening and the occasional game of cribbage.

Did she like him because of what he's done for her? Or for who he is? Hopefully the latter. Whatever happens now, his life was changed forever: he was a fugitive engaged with one of the most ruthless regimes in the world today, yet yesterday he was in ladies' underwear! *How did that happen?* he thought.

After three hours the ferry pulled into Dublin, and Morris and Sarah felt anxious as they slowly disembarked onto Irish soil.

'We must try to find a garage and a store that sells men's clothes. It's time to throw away the old Morris and bring on the new.'

Dublin in the sixties was a lively place, and they both enjoyed the hustle and bustle. They felt safe amongst the many shoppers going about their humdrum lives in O'Connell Street.

Ireland, like England, was slowly recovering after the war; there was a new energy in the shops, music and fashions.

There was a poster of Elvis in the music shops emblazoned with 'Hail the King'. Morris told Sarah that England had a new teen sensation like Elvis called Cliff Richard. Of course, the Irish had their own stars: Val Doonican, Ruby Murray, and The Bachelors.

Morris realised he only had sterling and was aware he was getting short of cash again. He was beginning to eat into his savings, which were going to buy a beach hut at Bognor Regis when he retired, but that seemed irrelevant now. He decided to go into a branch of Allied Irish to buy some Irish punts, roughly the same value as sterling.

The cashier explained he would have to phone the Reading central branch of Lloyds to verify his identity and that the account was in the black. After what seemed an age, the cashier returned and confirmed everything was in order.

They left the bank and Morris went into a men's outfitters, whilst Sarah went to a music shop.

'Good morning, sur,' said a young man in a suit.

'Oh, hello. I want some slacks or trousers, as you call them, a shirt and casual jacket.'

'Will it be for yourself, sur?'

'Well, yes.'

'Try these.' A pair of black trousers were produced on the counter.

'They are rather narrow legs,' said Morris.

'They are what we call drainpipes, sur – all the rage.'

'I think I prefer ordinary, thank you.'

The sales assistant put another pair on the counter. 'How about these?'

'But they're red,' said Morris.

'All the rage. Mick Jagger himself bought some of these whilst he was in Dublin.'

'Mick Jagger – eh, who's he?'

'*I can't get no satisfaction,*' said the shop assistant.

'Well,' said Morris, 'I don't think this is the time or place to discuss that.'

The shop assistant rolled his eyes and muttered something about an English dinosaur before asking, 'How about something in green?'

'Perfect, and perhaps a beige jacket with a pale blue shirt.'

'Tank you, sur,' said the Jagger man. 'That will be ten punts exactly.'

Morris gulped and handed over the correct notes. 'Do you have changing facilities?' he asked.

'Yes, sur, behind the curtain.'

'But it only comes halfway down,' said Morris.

'I know, sur. The other half is in changing room number two.'

'But,' said Morris, 'there is very little privacy.'

'I know, sur, but it has cut our shoplifting down one hundred per cent.'

Morris sheepishly went into the rather exposed changing room, removed his trousers and quickly put on the new ones. The shop assistant watched his every move. He changed his shirt and jacket, put his old clothes in the bag and left the shop.

Morris looked up and down the street but there was no sign of Sarah. He had been quite a long time, so he assumed she couldn't still be in the record shop. Morris became anxious wondering where she could be.

As he crossed the road, a car backfired and Morris hit the ground. *God, how did they follow me here?* He slowly lifted his face from the warm tarmac and felt a foot pushing him back down.

This is it, thought Morris, *shot dead on the main street in Dublin – just like in Hollywood westerns.*

'Hello, sweetie, it's only me,' said a female voice in a mock American tone.

Morris looked up to see it was Sarah wearing a plastic Elvis mask. 'What the hell are you doing?' he said.

'I bought an extended play forty-five rpm record and you get a free Elvis mask with every purchase,' she said, lifting the image of Elvis onto her forehead.

'You frightened the life out of me and look, I've got dust all over my new outfit.'

'Stand up –let me see.' She proceeded to brush him down just like Penelope did all those years ago.

'Gosh you look really smart,' said Sarah.
'I should think so, for what it cost me.'
'Come on, it's time to go.' They went back to the car parked in the newly built multistorey car park.

Chapter 14

As they left Dublin behind on the road to Cork, Morris asked Sarah had she heard of Michael Jagger. 'Apparently he's quite big in the charts, whatever they are.'

Sarah smiled and touched his arm. The Rover was getting dangerously low on petrol, so they made their way along empty winding roads heading south looking for a garage.

'Petrol 2 miles' said the sign. Morris gave a sigh of relief. As they drew near a large yellow Shell sign pinned to a tree came into view.

As he pulled onto the gravel forecourt a rather portly gentleman appeared.

'Good morro, sur. That is a pretty car, indeed it is.'

'It's black,' said Morris incredulously. 'Fill it up, please.'

'Indeed, sur,' said the rather plump garage proprietor, Morris assumed because there was no one else there.

When the pump had noisily delivered its contents, the garage man said, 'Step into my office, sur, and I will take your payment.'

Morris followed him into the shop. Sarah shouted she was going to use the bathroom facilities.

Morris stood at the counter handing over his cash with Irish music playing in the background when he saw that the shop sold sweets, ice creams and drinks.

'Is there anything else, sur?'

Morris looked around and focused on the ice cream cabinet.

'Help yourself, sur,' said the man.

Morris leant over into the cabinet and fished around for two suitable ice creams or lollies when the door suddenly burst open and a sallow-looking youth appeared in front of the counter.

'Give me all your money or I'll blow this place to smithereens!' he ordered.

Morris looked up somewhat startled and banged his head on the freezer cabinet lid. He was confronted with the youth who had a leather bag in one hand and a balaclava in the other.

Morris looked at him, then at his hand holding the balaclava and looked back at the yob. 'Shouldn't you be wearing that?' said Morris.

The youth looked at the balaclava and looked back at Morris. 'Oh shite, I knew I'd forget something,' he said. 'Here, hold this,' and proceeded to give Morris the leather briefcase while he put on the woollen hat. 'Don't drop it, there's a bomb ticking away inside,' he added matter-of-factly. 'I'll have it back now.'

'I don't think so,' said Morris before throwing it through the open door somewhere outside. Just then Sarah appeared wearing the Elvis mask.

'Oh, be jeebers,' said the would-be robber. 'I didn't know you were already robbing this place. Sorry, I'll be leaving you now.' He ran out, jumped on a motorbike and sped off down the road.

'I'll be thanking you for helping me,' said the garage man who had just stood there frozen to the spot, 'but I would rather he taken the money. He's the idiot son of Sean Reilly, leader of the local battalion of the IRA – it's a regular thing.'

'But you can't stand by and let people rob you,' said Morris.

'It's preferable to having my kneecaps and testicles removed,' he replied.

Morris had heard of the IRA, of course, but didn't realise they robbed their own. *But then again, how else could they buy guns and explosives from Czechoslovakia?* he mused.

'Good timing, Sarah,' said Morris, 'he thought you were robbing the shop as well. But what an idiot, he gave me the briefcase with the bomb inside while he— Oh my God. Quick, outside!'

They rushed outside but saw no sign of the bag.

'He must have taken it with him,' said Morris.

'Silly thing to do on a motorbike,' she said.

The garage man came out rather tentatively and advised Morris it might be better if they left as Sean Reilly may be paying him a visit soon, and garages selling petrol always burnt rather well.

Morris and Sarah jumped in the car and headed south.

'I bought you a present, Elvis.' Morris produced two ice lollies from the paper bag.

They found a lovely field overlooking a lake and sat there enjoying the orange-flavoured treats.

When they finished Morris tried to analyse quite what to do next, for not only were the KGB after him, but now probably the IRA as well. There they were in a black Rover 75, quite rare in Ireland, with English plates on it. *Fairly conspicuous,* he thought. *We only need the CIA and MI5 to get involved and we've got a full house! MI5 were probably on the lookout for Sarah anyway because she hadn't informed her father of her whereabouts, so he was probably a little concerned.*

Sarah leant over to the back seat of the car to retrieve the map. 'What's in the leather bag?' she asked.

'What leather bag?' said Morris.

She handed it over to the front. 'This black one.'

Morris slammed on the brakes and yelled, 'Get rid of it, now!'

'Why?' said Sarah, opening the clasp as curiosity got the better of her.

'It's a bomb! It's a bomb!'

Sarah had now fully opened it and looked at Morris who grabbed the bag, threw it out of the window, pulled Sarah's head down onto his lap and put his fingers to his ears.

Sarah was somewhat surprised by having her head forcibly pushed into Morris's crotch.

When there was no explosion, Morris pulled his fingers out of his ears and opened his eyes.

Sarah was still in the defensive position in his lap. Morris slowly pulled her upright.

'Slight overreaction,' said Sarah.

'The yob in the garage said it was a bomb and was due to go off any minute,' said Morris.

'Well, it felt like paper to me,' said Sarah.

They both looked out of the car window and saw the bag precariously balanced on a cliff edge overlooking a thirty feet drop down to the lake.

'Paper?' said Morris.

'Just paper, it felt like,' said Sarah.

They carefully stepped from the car and tiptoed towards the bag now tilting towards the drop.

'Quick, save it from going over the edge, Morris.'

'It…might…still be a bomb.'

'A bomb made of paper?' questioned Sarah.

Morris looked down slightly embarrassed, but he was a cautious man and risk had never been his strong point.

'Here, I'll get it,' offered Sarah.

'No,' said Morris, feeling a reluctant hero – but these things have to be done.

He was going to crawl on all fours but realising he had new trousers on, he thought it wasn't worth ruining them just for a bomb – and if it did explode the trousers would probably be soiled anyway, from inside.

Morris approached the bag wavering on the steep slope into the lake. If there was a hint of wind – not from Morris, but the climate – then it was gone forever.

Morris was curious as to why the Irish youth was carrying a bag full of paper, if it was paper. He was within two paces. *It was now or never,* he guessed.

He pounced on the bag and grappled with it like a ferret.

Suddenly, the cliff edge gave way and Morris gave way with it. With a shout, he was out of sight.

'Help,' came a muffled cry.

Sarah ran to the edge and saw a frantic Morris hanging in mid-air onto a branch rooted into the rock face. The bag fell from his grip and hit something solid. Not a splash, but Morris was too frightened to look down.

Sarah screamed, 'Morris, do something!'

'I am. I'm hanging on for dear life!'

'Have you got any rope in the car?' she asked.

'No, of course not. Find some cloth and tear it into strips,' he cried.

Sarah forgot about the sheet she had in one of her bags from the nurses' home and, undeterred, unbuttoned her dress and tore it to make a rescue rope.

'Here, grab this,' said Sarah lowering the end of her rolled-up dress.

Morris looked up and saw a woman in panties and bra lowering a blue floral dress for him to grab. He momentarily lost concentration, and then discovered the rescue rope wasn't long enough.

'Find something else, quickly,' he said.

Sarah rushed back to the car, rummaged through Morris's clothes on the back seat and found his pinstripe trousers. She then ran back to see Morris still hanging precariously above the water.

'Here, grab this,' she said lowering one leg of the trousers.

Morris grabbed it before looking up. 'Hey, these are my best trousers, they'll be ruined.'

'Shut up and grab it now.'

'But what will Mr Peabody of Jones and Jones say when I turn up in ripped pinstripe trousers?'

'Sod Mr Peabody! Hold on tight!' She tried to haul Morris up the cliff face holding the other trouser leg, but she wasn't strong enough. Inspiration then came to her. 'Stay there, Morris.'

'I wasn't going anywhere – I promise.' The branch he was hanging onto now began to bend and creak from his weight.

Sarah ran to the car and reversed it up to the ledge. She then tied the leather belt from the trousers tightly around the trouser leg and attached the other end to the bumper of the car. She jumped into the driver's seat and found reverse.

Much to Morris's dismay the 'make do' rescue rope slackened a little. 'The other way, stupid woman!'

'Don't call me stupid,' she whimpered before eventually finding first gear.

The car lurched forward dragging Morris up the cliff face into a shower of grit and dust as she spun the wheels.

He lay there silently for a moment, gradually wiping the dust from his face. He saw poor Sarah sitting in the driver's seat sobbing, dressed in only her underwear. She looked glorious.

Morris stood up and slowly walked towards the open door of the car. 'Jump out,' he said assertively.

Sarah slowly alighted from the seat and stood before him, still sobbing.

He opened his arms, grabbed her to him and wrapped his arms around her tightly. They both cried unreservedly.

He turned her cheek towards him and kissed her lips slowly and longingly; she held his head and kissed him back, like long-lost lovers.

After a few moments they both realised what was happening. Morris stood back. 'You'd better get dressed.'

'Yes, and look at your new clothes,' said Sarah.

Morris looked down. He was covered in grit and dirt and generally in a filthy state. *What a waste of ten punts' worth of clothing*, he thought.

Sarah went to the car and found a pair of jeans and a sweater while Morris brushed himself down.

He went to the rear of the car and untied the makeshift escape rope. His pinstripe trousers were split within three inches of coming apart altogether. Morris realised he was running out of clothing and wondered what to do.

'What happened to the bag?' asked Sarah.

'Oh, the bag, it fell and hit something. Let's look.'

They slowly approached the cliff edge and looked straight down the sheer rock face into the water.

'Oh, well, it's gone and good riddance,' said Morris.

They were about to retreat when Sarah noticed something white bobbing in the water under the cliff overhang.

'What's that down there? It looks like wood,' said Sarah.

Morris walked fifty yards to the left where the edge protruded further out. He could see it was a small fishing boat, and there, nestling in the bottom, was the black leather bag. *How strange,* thought Morris, *there's no mooring near here. It's very remote, so the boat must have broken its anchorage and ended up wedged under the cliff.*

'Sarah, quick, look. The bag is down there in the boat. To think I risked my life for that – but it's having a charmed life considering it's supposed to be a bomb.'

Sarah looked at Morris and clenched her teeth. 'Morris,' she said, 'there was something else in the bag under the paper – it felt like a gun. I didn't say so at the time to not alarm you.'

'Alarm me! Alarm me! I've got the KGB, the IRA and MI5 just around the corner, and probably the CIA no doubt, all trying to get a slice of me and you think I would be alarmed by the discovery of a gun in my car! Alarm me, whatever gave you that bloody idea?'

Morris found he was swearing quite a lot lately. He was now beginning to boil over and started stomping up and down.

Then, in the distance, he could hear the engine of a car coming. *Oh my God, which one of the pursuers is it?*

'Quick grab everything out of the car and hide in the trees over there,' he ordered pointing to a clump of fir trees and gorse.

Sarah gathered her bags. Morris just grabbed handfuls of whatever he thought useful, including the ignition key.

'What about Albert's cage?' said Sarah.

'Stuff Albert's cage, let's go!'

They ran to the cover of the trees and bushes and hid their belongings in the undergrowth just in time as the car came around the corner and pulled up sharply.

Four burly dark-haired men got out and surrounded the Rover.

'To be sure this is the one,' said one of the men.

Morris recognised him as the 'garage would-be robber'.

They looked around the car. Their thick Irish brogue was hardly recognisable as they talked amongst themselves.

Morris heard one say, 'Perhaps they got a lift, there's no keys. Michael, do your stuff.'

With that, Michael the mechanic got under the dashboard, took out a knife from his pocket and stripped the wires. He then rejoined them and the Rover started up.

'They're going to steal the car,' hissed Sarah. 'Do something!'

Morris looked confused. His mouth fell open but nothing came out.

One of the men ripped off the number plates and jumped in with Michael. The two cars disappeared up the road.

Morris looked at Sarah. Sarah looked at Morris.

'What now?' they said in unison.
'Bugger,' said Morris.
'Shit,' said Sarah.

Chapter 15

So, here were Morris and Sarah in the middle of southern Ireland being pursued possibly by every agency in the western world with just a few bedraggled belongings and no car.

'Shall we wait for a lift or find a farmhouse nearby?' asked Sarah.

'No, no, no,' said Morris. 'We don't want to arouse suspicion with anyone at the moment. Let me think.'

This strategic type of thinking was new to Morris and he found he was good at it. Analyse a situation, come up with alternatives and eliminate the ones that could get them into any more trouble.

'Right, we have some clothing, a bit of food, a map, ignition keys, but no car, an Elvis EP and a mask. My clothes are filthy and I think hanging over that cliff edge has soaked up all my antiperspirant,' said Morris.

It was late afternoon and fortunately a lovely summer's day with clear blue skies and just a few white clouds scurrying high above the lake.

'I think I'll have a scout around and see what's in the vicinity. You stay here and keep hidden, in case they come back,' Morris directed Sarah, who was beginning to like the assertiveness of Morris – it made him quite attractive.

Morris ventured further into the woods following an old disused path. When he reached the edge of the wood he took in his surroundings of fields and more fields, rolling with the landscape, with a backdrop of hazy mountains. *Quite breathtaking*, he thought to himself. It reminded him of his first motor holiday with Penelope in the Peak District staying in the Dovedale area at a bed and breakfast. Morris would walk miles every day after motoring to a designated starting point. Penelope stayed in the car knitting things for Stanley's feet, hands and head in rustic colours so as not to stand out – fat chance!

Morris could only see stone walls and little sign of habitation. *Even if it was inhabited, how safe would a somewhat bedraggled Englishman fare in these fiercely Republican areas? As an aside, everyone would surely know Sean Reilly, leader of the First Battalion IRA.*

Just as he was about to turn around and retrace his steps, he noticed a stone rooftop in a fold in the land about half a mile away. Keeping to the edges of the fields, sheltered by the stone walls, he made as direct a line as possible towards the slate rooftop. When he was nearly there, he crouched down under cover and slowly peeked through a hole in the wall. To his surprise, he saw an old chapel, obviously no longer used, but the roof was fairly sound.

He clambered down the bank and pushed open the door, which made a creaking noise similar to the horror movies he had seen at the cinema. There was a rustle and screeching as a large bird, perhaps an owl, made for the open door. Morris ducked down.

The contents of the chapel had been removed a long time ago. All that was left were a few pews and hymn books mouldy with age scattered around the floor. If it was raining, or winter, then he had found shelter; as it was, it was of little help in their current situation.

Morris noticed a small wooden cross on the floor. He picked it up, placed it on a pew and bowed. 'Please, God, help me out of this terrible mess I've got myself in. I appreciate you're probably only dealing with the Catholics in this area, but the other side need a fair crack of the whip as well, you know. We're almost the same, and forgive me my thoughts about Sarah. Hail Mary, Hail Mary, Hail Mary. Thank you.'

He made his way back towards the woods hoping Sarah was safe. He followed the path back to the tall trees and came to where he had left her.

She had gone, and all their belongings – not a trace.

Morris's mind went blank. *Had she been kidnapped or taken by some lunatic who had been watching their every move?*

Morris was distraught. He came out of the woods thinking, *what harm had befallen my, my...soulmate?* He wanted to say beloved, but it didn't sound right. He was married, he reminded himself, but he had never felt the pangs of misery in his stomach as he felt right now. His whole reason for being where he was, with half the world's hitmen after him, was no longer by his side.

He sat on a rock with his head in his hands and sobbed uncontrollably.

After a few minutes he heard, 'Morris, what's up, my love?'

Is that an angel I can hear? He looked up and there stood Sarah looking perfectly calm.

'Oh, Sarah, I thought they'd got you.' For the second time in the last hour he hugged her tight to his body, feeling her warm cheek next to his, and then kissed her passionately on the lips.

'Come with me, Morris, let me show you something,' she said.

She took his hand and led him around the side of the wood. There was a gate with wooden steps leading down the cliff to a sandy cove where all their worldly goods sat neatly stacked.

'Look, shelter.' She pointed to a cave at the back of the cove.

'How did you find this?' asked Morris.

'Well, you were gone some time, so I started to explore and found the steps. But, Morris, look behind you, over there. It's the boat under the cliff.'

Morris's eyes lit up, but then he realised it was two hundred yards away with very deep water in between and the wind was causing waves to lick at the hard rock face.

'We have no way of getting the boat,' said Morris. 'The tide never goes out from there.'

'There's no tide – it's a lake, Morris,' she said. Sarah looked disappointed hoping Morris would say he could swim out to retrieve the boat.

He saw her look and thought, *when was the last time I swam at all, let alone two hundred yards?* He suddenly remembered it was at school in the sports swimming gala and he was the anchorman in a 4 x 100 yard team event. He was in Ransome team. All the thirty-two teams were named after great authors: Wells, Shakespeare, Simpson, etc. Nobody had heard of the author Simpson, except the headmaster who insisted on the importance of including the unknown author. It later transpired R.J. Simpson was the headmaster's nom de plume and the author of rather racy novels. His work was certainly not available from your average bookshop, but sold from under the counter as per Lady Chatterley's Lover.

'Can you swim, Morris?'

'Yesssss,' he answered.

'If you can swim that far, then perhaps there'll be some oars in the boat and you can row back,' she said.

Not only was swimming a distant memory, so was rowing a boat.

Sarah put her arm around him and said, 'What you've been through the last two days, you can do anything, my love.' She then added, 'Take your clothes off.'

'Why do I have to take my clothes off?' questioned Morris.

'Then I can wash them for you in the water. They'll soon dry with the warm breeze coming off the lake. After all, I took my clothes off for you!'

'That was an emergency, and I didn't look once,' he lied.

'This is our only chance, Morris. You can do it.'

Morris stripped down to his underpants and dipped his toe in the water. It was freezing.

'And those,' she said pointing to his underpants.

'Now, wait a moment,' said Morris. 'That's going a bit too far.'

'Oh for God's sake! I'm a nurse. I've seen it all before.'

'A trainee nurse, no hard-core stuff,' said Morris defensively.

'Off,' she commanded.

'If I get frostbite, I will never forgive you.'

'Well, in that case, you'll be no good to me anyway,' she said laughing.

Morris looked surprised and thought he had misheard what she'd said. He slowly lowered his pants and cupped his hand between his legs protecting his vital organs.

'Go on, then. It'll be dark soon.'

Morris let out a loud whoop, ran to the water's edge and dived in. His white body stood out in the dark water as he recalled how to swim. At first he tried overarm, but found that tiring, so he converted to breaststroke and headed for the boat.

There was a swell in the lake, and Morris found it like swimming against the tide. He was making slow progress and found himself drifting further out away from the rock face. His breathing became very heavy as he struggled. Looking back at Sarah standing there waving, he knew he had to do it for her. It was the first time he had swam in the nude and found the experience quite invigorating.

There were the remains of a wooden structure sticking up in the lake, possibly a mooring stake, so Morris held onto that for a while to regain some air in his lungs. A few minutes later he made one last desperate attempt to reach the boat.

Sarah was concerned and looked at her watch. He had been gone for forty-five minutes. In that time she had rinsed his clothes and spread them out on the rocks to catch the last of the warm breeze.

Morris reached out for the side of the boat thinking it would pull away from the rock face, but it seemed fixed. He hauled himself on board and sat on the crossbench to see what the boat had in terms of equipment. There were two oars and the black bag lying on the bottom of the boat and, to his surprise, an outboard motor. The boat was tightly wedged under a cleft in the rocks, so he tried pushing with his hands, but to no avail. He then tried with the oars pushing against the rock face, but it wouldn't budge. Morris thought the only way to dislodge it was if he could get under the front of the boat and pull it down causing the rock to release the front end.

Morris had never swam underwater before but it was called for, so he took a deep breath and jumped over the side holding his nose. He worked his way to the front end and tugged with all his might. There was slight movement, but he had to come up for air. He took another big breath and went down again. This time the boat came away, and Morris rose through the water. He felt the boat float freely away from the rocks. He clambered back on board and in the process painfully caught his tackle on one of the rowlocks. He winced to himself, forgetting that he was completely naked.

He pushed away from the rocks with an oar wondering whether the outboard motor was working and if there was any fuel. It was just a small British Seagull engine, usually used for manoeuvring about rather than major excursions. He pulled it upright, lowered it slowly over the stern of the boat and clamped it to the backboard. He opened the fuel tank and sure enough there was half a tank full, so he pulled the starting rope, but there wasn't even a splutter. He tried six times but to no avail. On the seventh try it struggled to fire up, but with a gurgle and a cough it roared into life.

He turned the boat around and made for the cove, which only took a few minutes to reach. He stood up on the seat cheering, completely oblivious to his nakedness, when he approached Sarah. He pulled the vessel onto the shore, and Sarah gave him a big hug and a pair of pants. He suddenly looked down and realised he was as nature intended. Feeling self-conscious, he quickly retrieved his dignity with newly washed underwear. Morris thought, *all these years talking ladies' underwear, yet I'm still self-conscious when only dressed in underwear.*

Morris was exhausted. Sarah found some biscuits retrieved from the car and they sat pondering their next move. They decided to have a good night's sleep and start fresh in the morning.

They walked towards the cave and gathered what clothes they could to make some sort of bedding.

'Goodnight, Sarah.'

'Goodnight, Superman,' said Sarah, smiling at her hero.

It was quite chilly, and she moved closer to him.

He put his arm around her and drew her closer, their bodies touching.

Morris went into a deep sleep thinking, *I must phone Penelope tomorrow – there's always tomorrow.*

They slept peacefully apart from when Morris woke a couple of times and caught glimpses of Sarah's face from the moonlit sky. He brushed her hair away from her eyes and settled down once again.

Chapter 16

Morris was awake at daybreak and longed for a coffee and toast to start the day, but there were only digestive biscuits. He dressed in his newly rinsed clothes and started to put their goods in the boat. His watch said five thirty; the early morning mist hovered above the surface of the lake.

He shook Sarah. She turned over and opened her eyes, wider and wider, not expecting to see the scene before her. The sea, the rocks, Morris and a boat – *am I dreaming?*

When Morris moved the oars he saw the black bag that was reminiscent of a doctor's bag. The black bag that nearly caused his death yesterday. He still looked at it with some contempt but moved it onto the seat and gently undid the clasp. Opening it cautiously he peered into the contents and stood back in amazement. He lurched forward again and had another look. Irish pound notes of all denominations; possibly thousands of them.

'Sarah, come here quickly.'

Sarah gathered her slip-on shoes and ran across to the boat where Morris stood motionless.

'Look in the bag,' he said.

Sarah clambered aboard and leant forward to see why Morris was so excited.

'Wow,' she said. 'Where did you get those from? There's thousands.'

'I didn't get them – they were just there in the bag. It must have been the proceeds of the young garage robber's previous jobs. That's why they came looking for us and took the car.'

'What should we do?' said Sarah, grabbing handfuls of five, ten and twenty punt notes. Her hand reached lower in the bag and felt something cold and hard. 'Morris, it's the gun lying on the bottom.'
'What-what-what sort of gun?'
'The handgun, revolver,' said Sarah.
'Oh Christ.' The nearest Morris had been to a gun was during the Second World War in Aldershot, but he was in the catering corps, so weapons were not a priority. He had used a fire extinguisher once to put out a fat fryer. *Probably similar,* he thought.

It was getting lighter and it was time for decisiveness. Morris surmised the money was stolen using the gun of a young Sean Reilly, therefore, he wasn't the rightful owner. Morris convinced himself that it was good it was no longer in his hands and would like to return the money to its lawful owners. *But who were they?*
Sarah was busy counting the cash and putting it into neat piles. When she finished she let out a yell. 'Nine hundred Irish pounds,' she called out breathlessly. 'This is a gift from heaven,' she exclaimed, 'all our problems are over. We can buy a car, get the ferry back to England and go back to our old lifestyle.'
'What do you mean? Keeping the money would be theft. I think we should take the boat across the water and find a village to call the police.'
'Are you mad?' screamed Sarah 'Even the Garda are corrupt in this country and probably all friends with Sean Reilly, or any other member of the IRA.'
Morris sat down on the seat and rested his head in his hands. He confessed he had never taken anything that wasn't his in his life.
'But it was going to those crooks for drugs, crime and prostitution,' said Sarah.

Morris thought, *that's true, and drugs destroys lives.* Stanley told him that just before driving off in his brand new Ford Zodiac.

Crime, well, Morris had been a law-abiding citizen all his life, yet what does he get in return? Some youths stealing his plastic gnome with a fishing rod in the front garden of his house in Berkshire – bastards. And prostitution, well, Morris thought there was a girl in Romford once he met in a pub. When she asked for payment upfront, Morris gave her a pair of his best quality knickers in triple XL, which she took as an insult. She got up and left, leaving Morris holding a pair of knickers in full view of everyone in the pub.

'OK,' said Morris, 'I agree, it's ours. Finders keepers. Let's go.'

Morris fitted the Seagull motor over the side and gave it one mighty pull. It fired up immediately. He steered the boat out of the bay and took stock of the lake and surrounding land. It was man-made he decided, therefore, probably a reservoir, so there must be a control room over the dam with occupants watching water levels and reading newspapers.

Sarah sat quietly tying the notes into bundles with some string she had found. The little boat ploughed on through the choppy expanse of water when Morris saw the grey walls of the dam with castellated towers at each end. *There will be a walkway or a road on top of the wall allowing passage from one side to the other,* he reckoned.

It must have been half a mile to the wall. Morris steered straight at it sensing civilisation and contact with normal mankind.

The boat bounced along the tops of the waves, when two hundred yards from the dam the engine spluttered and came to a halt. It had run out of petrol.

'Bugger,' said Morris.

'Damn,' said Sarah, smiling at her clever little joke.

'We'll have to row the rest of the way,' said Morris. 'Can you row?'

'A little at university,' said Sarah.

'Good, then I'll steer.'

'Whoa! I can't row this on my own. Here take an oar.' She beckoned Morris to sit and start rowing.

Initially it was a bit uneven as Sarah was a much stronger oarsperson. The boat ended up going round in circles.

'Big breath and relax. Watch.' She demonstrated a perfect technique and told Morris to follow her, but it wasn't necessary; the boat aimed towards the dam walls on its own, as if being pulled.

'Oh my God,' said Sarah. 'We've got into the undercurrent where the water is drawn into the turbos that drive the generator to produce electricity.'

'I could do without the engineering lesson,' said Morris. 'What do we do?'

They were just yards from the grey dam wall. Up on the parapets passers-by had noticed the small craft well within the safety buoys of the dam.

They both realised they were in trouble. It was probably thirty feet from the top of the water, up the wall and onto the walkway.

A man in uniform wearing a captain's hat threw over a rope and life buoy for Morris to catch.

He missed it several times before Sarah helped.

'Climb up the ropes,' said the captain.

Morris looked at Sarah and they defiantly shouted, 'No!'

'Pull the rope along the road, away from the central channel,' shouted Sarah.

They were not going to risk everything for their precious cargo: an Elvis EP record, a mask, some clothing and a black bag.

The captain started to walk along the pathway holding the rope, but the current was too strong. Other men joined in and gradually they made progress away from the central area of the dam.

Morris and Sarah helped by using the oars. Having tied the rope on the front, they used the oars to push away the boat from the solid walls.

Eventually they reached the landing stage and tied the boat to a post, and then clambered onto the wooden jetty. Meanwhile, the captain and friends came running down the steps.

'Why didn't you leave the boat and climb the walls on the ropes?' asked one of them.

'You could have been drawn under with the force of the central channel,' said the captain.

'Bad leg,' said Morris, 'an old war wound I picked up in Belgium.'

Sarah coughed, and they thanked everyone for their help. By this time the local newspaper had sent someone out following a phone call from the tower.

Morris put all the contents of the boat on the jetty and was about to walk towards the main building when the newspaper lad said, 'Smile,' and took a picture of Morris and Sarah holding a bundle of clothing and a black bag.

'I can see the headline now,' said the photographer, '"Dam-n close call".'

'You can't use the picture,' said Morris, 'we work for the government and are undercover.'

'But that's the UK government, it has no jurisdiction here, my boyo,' said the newspaperman who then ran off with his scoop.

Morris and Sarah walked towards the tower and climbed some steps into the office, which was situated high above the dam with wonderful views in all directions.

'That was a rather silly thing to do,' said the man behind the desk. 'People have died doing what you did.'

'We didn't know. We just pulled out into the lake and found ourselves being drawn by the current towards the dam,' said Sarah.

'Oh, you're English, are you? But you have a slight accent,' said the man behind the desk. 'What are you doing in these parts?'

'Sightseeing. Looking at chapels and churches and logging them,' said Morris.

'Why would you be doing that now?'

'I belong to the Berkshire Spire Appreciation Society,' said Morris. 'We like to see interesting spires in other countries.'

'We're all Catholic and chapel is good enough for the folk round here. We don't need fancy spires to call the congregation to prayer.'

Sarah noticed a picture of the gentleman with the inscription 'Presented to Patrick Rafferty to Commemorate 25 Years as Lay Preacher to the District'.

'Could I use your phone?' said Morris.

'You can if you pay for it,' said Mr Rafferty. 'There's one in the lobby.'

Morris left the room and found the phone. He picked up the receiver and a woman's voice said, 'This is the exchange. Which number would you like?'

'Reading 29978, please?' said Morris.

There was silence for a moment before suddenly Penelope's voice said, 'Hello.'

'Penny, it's me.' Morris never called her Penny. 'How are you? Sorry I missed a call last night, but I'm in Ireland, southern Ireland.' There was a short pause and he frowned. 'Yes, it is a long way from Telford. Mr Squires wanted me to attend a trade fair in Dublin, so I continued my journey across Wales and I'm now here in Dublin. He thinks there'll be foreign buyers there looking for English cotton garments. How's the garden?' Another pause as he listened to her reply. 'Good – did you put the dustbin out? This time of year it smells if you forget.'

A voice cut in, 'Have you finished yet?'

'Yes, almost,' said Morris. 'Penny, what's today? Oh, Wednesday. I should be home at the weekend – hopefully get a game of bowls in.' He waited for her response before saying, 'See you soon, bye.'

Click. The phone went dead.

'Was that your wife now,' said the woman's voice at the exchange.

'It was. Were you listening?'

'Accidentally forgot to switch off my headphones, sur. You may have told a tiny porky there, sur, as you're not in Dublin but in a village about a hundred miles from Dublin. But, still, she won't be able to know now, will she, sur? Good day to you, sur.'

Morris returned to the office where Mr Rafferty and Sarah were getting on like a house on fire making a cup of tea and slicing a piece of malted loaf.

'One of the lads tells me you're on government business when you're not looking for spires. How's the bad leg?'

Morris limped across the room desperate for a cup of tea, they hadn't eaten properly since yesterday, and he scoffed down the fresh bread.

Sarah looked at him and intimated to calm down with her eyes.

'What sort of government business then, Mr...'

'Leyland,' said Morris. 'Mark Leyland.'

'So, Mr Leyland, you're on holiday with your...' He looked across to Sarah.

'My daughter,' said Morris. 'Yes, we often go on holiday and leave the little lady at home to look after the ferrets. That's who I called just now to check they're all OK.'

'Oh yes, that'll be one punt for the call,' said Mr Rafferty.

Morris opened his wallet and showed he was carrying a lot of cash transferred from the black bag.

'Here's a five Irish punt note. That's for the calls, tea and bread. Could you make one more call for a taxi to take us to the nearest station?'

Mr Rafferty looked at the money and was somewhat overwhelmed by Morris's generosity. 'Indeed I will. Mr Leyland – you say. I'll use the phone in the lobby. Mary at the exchange knows a local taxi man. He'll be here very soon to be sure.'

After he left the room Sarah whispered, 'I don't like this man, Morris, he's shifty.'

Sarah moved closer to the door and could hear Mr Rafferty saying in a hushed voice, 'I'm pretty sure it's them... You say a man and a girl. That's definitely what they are, a man and girl, and he's carrying a lot of cash with him... Wait for it – a black bag with "S.R." on the side... OK, you'll send a special taxi for them straightaway... Thank you. Bye, Sean. God be with you.'

They spent five uncomfortable minutes pacing the floor. Morris was exaggerating his new limp when a car turned up and sounded its hooter.

Morris and Sarah gathered their stuff, left the dam offices and were then met by a large dark-haired man.

'Let me help you with your things, madam,' he said.

Sarah let him put her belongings in the boot. Morris held onto the little black bag. They climbed into the car and sat back.

'Where would you be going?' asked the driver.

'Nearest mainline station, please. We want to go to Cork.'

'Right you are.'

Morris sat tightly holding the bag; Sarah held his other hand. The car reversed out of the yard and proceeded to go up a ramp that took them onto the roadway along the dam wall.

Morris thought this was strange. He caught the driver looking at him in his rearview mirror; he realised it was Michael, the mechanic, who hot-wired his Rover. He was taking them back to yesterday's side of the lake and probably Sean Reilly and his family.

Morris tightly squeezed Sarah's hand. She looked at him and followed his eyes to the back of the driver's head. She then looked in the rear view mirror and could see it was Michael.

They reached the concrete road at the end of the dam and entered the highway going west. Morris looked apprehensive.

Sarah suddenly shouted, 'I'm going to be sick. Quick, stop the car!'

Michael, not wanting projectile vomit down his neck, pulled over in a gate entrance. 'Quick, get out,' he ordered.

Sarah threw open the car door, ran towards a stone wall and gave the impression she was throwing up.

Very convincing, thought Morris.

Michael stood between her and the car while Morris quietly leant over and took the keys from the ignition. He then proceeded to open the black bag and produced the gun.

'Move towards the gate,' said Morris to Michael, who stood with a look of horror on his face.

'Yes, sir, yes,' he said.

Sarah stood up from her prone position and ran towards Morris.

'See if there's any rope in the car.'

Sarah opened the boot and found some rope.

'Hold the gun on him while I tie him up.' Morris then proceeded to tie Michael to the five-bar gate using knots he remembered from his service days when tying down cattle before slaughter, which he hated, but he was rather enjoying this latest episode.

When Morris had secured him to the gate, he released the catch and let the gate swing inward taking Michael heavily against the inside of the wall, where he couldn't be seen from the road.

'Quick, in the car,' said Morris.

He put the keys in the ignition and started the motor.

'Where to now?' asked Sarah.

'Well, we can't go back over the dam, they might recognise the car. We have to go west, and then south towards Cork.'

'Morris, you saved me again. You're my real-life hero,' said Sarah. 'I shall never forget you whatever happens after this.' She kissed him on the cheek and squeezed his arm.

Morris stopped the car and pulled over. He leant towards her and their lips met in a passionate embrace.

'In some ways I hope this never ends, but we're in danger and must get back to England,' he said softly. As he pulled away from her embrace, his hand touched her breasts and he felt the soft skin through her shirt. 'I'm sorry,' said Morris, retreating to his driver's side.

'Come here,' said Sarah. She slowly unbuttoned her satin top and took Morris's hand placing it on her breast. She turned towards him. They kissed more passionately, more than Morris thought he was capable of, and her breast was the softest, sweetest thing he had ever touched.

They heard a tractor coming along the lane and although Morris wanted to stay like this forever, he quickly looked in the rearview mirror. He pulled out just in front of the tractor and sped down the road.

It must have been twenty minutes before either of them spoke a word.

'It's clouding over,' said Sarah.

'Yes,' said Morris, 'we need to find a main road and get to Cork before dark.'

Sarah read the map and they found themselves back on the main road and headed south. The hills rode by in the background along with field after field of green, green fields bordered by stone walls containing grazing cattle and sheep.

Chapter 17

Morris thought of Penny. *What was she doing? It's Wednesday, so it's crib afternoon. Oh good, she'll be busy cooking cakes in preparation for her usual guests.* Then his train of thought changed. *I wonder if we've got a home fixture in the bowls league on Sunday? Oh God, what about Mr Squires?* Morris's mind was racing. *I need to tell him how I'm getting on, but I have no sales. Perhaps I can find a shop in Cork that could justify my coming here. And what about the Rover? It belonged to the company, a sort of hand-me-down from Mr Squires himself. How do I explain its disappearance? I don't even know what I'm driving now.* He looked at the car's dash. *Oh, it's a Wolseley,* he concluded seeing the badge on the steering wheel. *Not a bad swap,* he thought.

He looked at Sarah and smiled. She smiled back.

It was late afternoon and both were hungry so they decided to seek out a hotel. *This car has Irish plates, so it should be safe here and won't arouse suspicion,* he thought to himself.

They entered the town of Cork and saw a sign for 'County Hotel'.

'Looks posh and expensive,' said Sarah.

'Great,' said Morris, 'we've got plenty,' he added remembering the little black bag. 'What was it, nine hundred Irish punts, I believe?'

They pulled onto the car park and parked up next to the other cars, gathered their stuff and bags, which were looking a little worse for wear now, and entered the hotel lobby.

'Good evening, madam and sir,' said the receptionist. 'How may I help you?'

'Do you have any vacancies?' said Morris.

'Yes, what did you require?'

'A double,' said Sarah, pushing forward and elbowing Morris out of the way.

'That's fine. You can have the suite overlooking the river. Do you need help with your luggage?' she said, curiously looking at their odd collection of baggage.

'No – it's fine,' said Morris.

'Second floor, room ten. The lifts are over there.'

The interior of the hotel was rich in polished wood and glass and had probably seen many famous faces staying there whilst visiting this fine old city.

The lift stopped and Morris and Sarah alighted onto a corridor with scenic prints on the walls and expensive carpets on the floor. They found their room, opened the door and found it rather pleasant with a full size window opening onto a balcony overlooking the River Lee. They dropped their bags and stood watching the few fishing boats on the river and pleasure boats with families enjoying the trip.

'I need a shower,' said Sarah.

'I think I'll catch the shops before they close to buy some more clothes and perhaps find a likely client for some sales tomorrow,' said Morris.

He left the hotel and wandered towards the shops looking in wonderment at the brightly painted houses. He walked by the harbour and back into town where he found a men's clothes shop. He bought a shirt and trousers with some of the money from the bag and a new pair of brogues in brown and white.

He had never felt so young and invigorated, but he knew shortly that it would all have to end. Tomorrow they would have to catch a ferry from Cork to Swansea, make a stop at Swansea, see an old customer, and then go back to leafy Berkshire.

He strolled back to the hotel and found a phone in the lobby.

'Hello, Mr Squires, please.'

'Morris, how are you? How's your Irish trip going?'

'Oh, pretty quiet. Not too much happening.'

'Oh, no sales, then?'

'On the contrary,' said Morris. 'I visited a trade fair in Dublin and sold two hundred pairs of the Holdall range to a wholesaler, and I gave him a discount if he paid upfront. Hundred and fifty Irish pounds. I'll come up next week with the money.'

'Two hundred pairs! Morris, you're a true salesman. How's the Rover going, by the way?'

'Ah, well, it was giving me trouble, so I traded it in for a rather nice Wolseley. I will have to re-register it when I get back home, but I think you'll like it.'

'Look forward to seeing you. Bye,' said Mr Squires.

Morris put more coins in the phone box.

'Hello, Penny... How are things? Yes, I'm fine, in Cork at a trade convention... Going well... You cooking for your guests this evening? Good... I'm in a bed and breakfast and will probably have a meal, and then listen to the radio, although they have TV, but not sure I can handle too much excitement... Will possibly be back on Friday... See you... Enjoy your evening.'

He put the phone down having done his duty.

Morris made his way back to the room where he was greeted by Sarah with a towel wrapped around her body.

'Enjoy your walk? What have you bought?'

'Wait and see.' Morris went into the bathroom and had a good wash and shaved off two days' worth of stubble. He found some smelly stuff on the shelf and put on his new clothes.

'Da-da,' he said flinging open the door and presenting himself to her.

Sarah was lying on the bed with the towel loosely draped across her body.

Morris looked across the room and strolled over to the balcony. He stopped just inside the window and looked out at the setting sun reflecting off the glass roof lights to avoid looking at Sarah.

'I've phoned my boss and told him I've had a big sale in Dublin.'

He heard movement, and then two soft arms embraced him from behind. He stood there while her head rested on his shoulder. He turned to behold the most beautiful sight he had ever seen. She was naked and stood there with her hands on her hips for Morris to take in this wondrous sight.

She drew him towards her and slowly unbuttoned his new shirt before kissing him on the lips. Her hands hurriedly undressed him. Soon he, too, was naked. She then turned and walked to the bed beckoning him with her finger.

Morris remembered he'd seen a movie in the early days with Errol Flynn running and leaping onto a fair maiden's bed. Morris stepped back two or three steps, and then tripped on the threshold. He landed out on the balcony flat on his back, completely naked.

He looked up rather sheepishly and found he was being observed by an elderly couple on the next balcony and a guy on the other side.

Morris stood up holding his hand between his legs to preserve his dignity when there was a sudden cheer below from a boat full of schoolchildren.

'Oh, shit,' said Morris and ran back in to find Sarah creased up with laughter sitting on the side of the bed.

'My hero!' she cried.

By now, all manly desire had left his body and his dignity with it. He gathered his clothes and tried to dress quickly when there was a knock on the door.

'Everything all right, sir?' said a man in a porter's uniform.

'Yes, fine. Why?'

'We've had reports of a disturbance from a couple in room eleven and an enquiry from a gentleman in room nine asking whether you are travelling alone.'

'We're fine, thank you.'

'Good evening, sir.'

Morris shut the door and found Sarah fully dressed and smiling.

'Let's find a restaurant and blow some serious cash,' she enthused.

Morris had never blown 'serious cash' before and wasn't quite sure how one goes about it.

Chapter 18

They walked arm in arm down to the harbour side and found a restaurant with outside seating overlooking the water. They were taken to a table with candles and flowers in a vase.

'Let's go for it. The most expensive food on the menu – lobster, crab, foie gras, the best wine on the list,' said Sarah. 'Tonight we celebrate our relationship and undying respect for each other.'

She didn't say 'love', Morris thought. Perhaps just as well. How could you love someone like me? A middle-aged married man who sells knickers. Wait a minute, she doesn't know I'm married. I told her... No. When she asked... Oh well, best she doesn't know, he concluded.

As the night progressed, with the lights sparkling on the water, there came a sudden sound of a piano from inside the restaurant. *Oh no,* thought Morris, *not again.*

They wandered through the streets after the meal and looked in every shop window pointing out things just for the sakes of it and laughing at each other.

Morris excused himself when they returned to the hotel while Sarah collected the key and climbed the stairs. Morris waited until she was out of sight and then made for the bar in the lounge. After exchanging pleasantries with the barman he downed two glasses of Irish whisky. Unaccustomed as he was to drinking, he felt ready to take on whatever the world threw at him tonight.

He took the lift to level two and knocked on the door of, unwittingly by mistake, room nine in the dimly lit corridor.

'It's not locked, come in,' came a rather put-on voice.
What the hell is going on in our room? Where's Sarah? Have they traced us here? Morris kicked open the door and saw a well-dressed young man sitting on the bed.

'Where's Sarah?' he said lunging forward and taking the man's throat in both hands and wrestling with him on the bed.

'Like a bit of rough stuff, do we? OK, here goes,' said the mystery occupant who then put Morris in a headlock, threw him on the floor and they rolled across the floor towards the window.

'Oh, this is fun. I can't wait to make up,' and with that he threw Morris once more over his shoulder and went out through the open window onto the balcony where Morris rattled against the metal railings and slumped into a heap.

'OK, big boy, bedtime.' Just as the young man was about to pick him up there came a cry from the adjacent balcony.

'Morris!'

'Sarah,' said Morris breathlessly, 'are you OK? What are you doing in that room?'

'This is our room, Morris. You're in the wrong room. You're in room nine with that young man, or whatever he is.'

'Careful, sweetie,' said the young guy. 'I didn't know he was spoken for. You can have him – he's very old.'

With that, Morris got to his feet, took a swing at the young man and flattened him. 'Nice to meet you. We must do it again sometime.' Morris wrung his hands and left the room somewhat ruffled but satisfied.

He then entered room ten to a startled Sarah who remarked, 'What is it about you that seems to find trouble, Morris?'

'Just unlucky, that's all,' he said nonchalantly.

Chapter 19

They lay there staring at the ceiling.

'Well, we've got a long trip tomorrow, we'd better get some rest,' said Sarah.

They discreetly undressed in their respective areas. Morris realised he hadn't bought any new pyjamas, apart from the old-fashioned striped ones he always wore. *Not very becoming,* he thought.

Sarah looked up from the sheets and said quietly, 'Come on, darling. I won't look, I promise. After all, I've seen it all before.'

Morris made sure he kept to the shadows in the room with just the moonlight creating a window pattern on the carpet.

She threw back the covers inviting Morris to join her.

He slowly sat on the bed and put one leg in, and then the other before quickly pulling up the covers. As his legs slowly straightened, he could feel the soft skin of her thighs as they lay on their backs.

'Look at me, Morris,' she commanded.

He turned to see the moonlight outlining the beautiful features of her face. He touched her nose with his finger, then her lips, the hollow of her neck, and then he stopped.

'I want you to, Morris,' she said softly.

Just then Morris heard a noise on the balcony. He opened his eyes and looked through the window where he saw two legs dangling down. He pushed back the covers and slowly crept over. There, hanging on a rope, was Michael 'the mechanic' looking up instructing Sean to lower the rope further.

'A bit more,' he whispered.

'That's all there is.'

'Another ten feet, that's all,' whispered Michael even louder. 'Get a longer one.'

'I'll have a look,' said Sean who let go of the rope and walked away.

Michael fell onto the balcony with a bang.

Morris, still naked, fell onto a dazed Michael and wound the rope around his body.

Sarah ran to the window covered in only a sheet. 'What on earth?' she said.

'They've traced us here in Cork and must've seen the car parked up,' said Morris.

'What now?' said Sarah.

'Time for a swim,' and with that Morris hauled Michael upright and lifted his legs over the railings. With an almighty heave he threw him over the top into the river.

Just then, another piece of rope appeared above their heads from the darkness of the roof.

'Here, Michael, grab this, it's longer. It reaches right up here and I've tied it around me waist.'

Sarah looked at Morris and together they pulled the rope and then heard an almighty, 'Mary, mother of Christ!' Sean tumbled past the balcony and he, too, made a mighty splash.

The lights went on from rooms nine and eleven. The elderly couple once again came out onto the balcony and saw a naked Morris and Sarah wearing only a sheet.

'What's with you English?' said the woman.

'You need treatment,' said the young man in room nine, 'constantly parading around naked. You're a naughty boy.'

With that Morris and Sarah closed the windows and sat in silence on the bed.

'Bloody inconvenient, I was about to—'

'Shush,' said Sarah, putting her fingers to his lips.

'Huh,' said Morris. He lay there facing the ceiling contemplating his bad luck and loss of the greatest moment of his life as Sarah cuddled in behind him.

'Goodnight, my hero,' she said.

Chapter 20

They woke at seven o'clock and the rain was thundering down as it only can in Ireland. The harbour looked deserted and forlorn.

They got dressed and went down for breakfast. When he paid the bill the amount nearly made him choke. *But what the heck, it's not my money,* he thought.

As they packed their stuff in the car Morris realised that somewhere in Cork was a Rover with two hundred pairs of double gusset knickers for the discerning woman. *Perhaps the IRA will find a use for them. Replacement sandbags, headgear, potato gatherers – who knows?*

They made their way to the ferry and drove on board making a mental note it was goodbye to Ireland and hello Wales.

The trip to Swansea was going to take hours, so Morris and Sarah sat in the car and talked about their series of adventures and what they meant to them individually.

Sarah expressed her admiration for Morris being a gentleman and helping in the first place, and then getting involved with the KGB and IRA all because of her.

She said she never believed he was an international businessman from the start, but she enjoyed his imagination and the lifestyle as he told her at the beginning.

Morris, on the other hand, said how much his new view of life had changed and how he'd become more positive and daring and had a can-do attitude now, which he credited her with for making him into a person he had only seen in the cinema.

He took her hand in his and held it to his chest. He was about to confess that perhaps he was a little bit in love with her when there was a loud blast from the ship's siren announcing they were approaching Swansea.

The ferry tied up alongside the jetty and they disembarked. It was mid-afternoon and the rain had cleared. Morris said he needed to visit a store in the city centre to pay a courtesy call on King, Goodman and Baker –Wales's biggest department store.

When they parked behind the store Morris suggested Sarah look around the clothing department and spend some money as there was a considerable amount still in the little black bag.

He tidied his clothes and realised he'd lost his tie somewhere in Ireland, so he quickly went to the men's department and bought a striped little number and pinstripe trousers befitting an international businessman.

He knocked on the door of the chief buyer, Mr Alwyn Evans, whom he had known for many, many years.

'Ah, Morris. How are you?' said Mr Evans.

'Oh, pretty much the same. Nothing changes in ladies' underwear.'

'How's the good wife? Penelope, isn't it?' said Mr Evans.

'Fine,' said Morris with a tinge of guilt. 'I'm looking forward to getting home tomorrow. Perhaps a game of bowls on Sunday.'

Mr Evans explained that the store was being hit by chain stores and they needed to modernise with a new image and layout. An advertising company suggested shortening the name to make it catchier.

'KGB,' said Mr Evans.

Morris ducked down by the desk covering his ears waiting for the blast of a gun.

'What on earth are you doing, Morris?'

Morris looked around realising his overreaction. 'Oh... King, Goodman and Baker – KGB. Do you think that's wise?' he asked.

'Well, we don't think people around here will think we're headquarters for the Russian secret service.'

'Why not just call it Kings? It's short and portrays the modern image you want to project.'

'Kings... Kings Store. Kings, fit for royalty,' said Mr Evans. 'I like it, especially as young Mr King is the only real family member alive now! Good, Morris, I will put it to the board at our next meeting. Now, about that order you wanted. It was for fifty pairs, wasn't it?'

Morris looked surprised as he'd never had an order that big from King, Goodman and Baker, or KGB or Kings, before.

'I will phone it through on Monday,' said Morris, 'and thank you. I'll see you in a few weeks' time. Bye.'

They shook hands, and Morris left the office feeling really pleased with himself. He walked through the store and down two floors when he saw Sarah at the jewellery counter.

'Hi, darling,' she said, making Morris feel proud and young and vibrant again.

'What are you looking at?' said Morris. 'How about a gold chain with a heart suspended from it? The best one they have.' He got the attention of the assistant. 'Excuse me, miss, how much is this chain?'

'It is our best one, sir. Is it for the young lady? It's really beautiful, isn't it? It's only twenty pounds.'

'Wrap it up,' said Morris. 'No, wait. Let's put it on.' He turned to Sarah who stood there motionless, if not a little embarrassed.

Morris placed the gold chain with heart around her neck. As he touched her skin it brought back the memory of her naked body standing in front of him the previous night.

'Cash or cheque, sir?'

This request brought Morris out of his daydream. He produced twenty Irish pounds.

'I'm not sure we can accept these, sir.'

Morris suddenly realised he had a wallet full of Irish punts, and no sterling. 'Damn.'

'Here, I've got some money,' said Sarah producing the appropriate note as she'd changed some punts into sterling whilst shopping.

'Thank you, madam. Not such a surprise any more, is it?' said the assistant sarcastically and looking at Morris with disdain.

They quickly left and Morris suggested they find the car and transfer the money from the black bag. They found a bank and placed the bag on the counter.

'Could you exchange five hundred Irish pounds sterling, please?' said Morris confidently.

The male cashier looked at the money and said, 'For such a large amount I'll have to get the manager.' He quickly went to the back of the office and returned with a middle-aged, balding man.

'This is a very large amount to exchange, sir,' said the manager.

'Yes, it is,' said Morris. 'I'm thinking of transferring my clothing company from Ireland to Wales. Better access to international markets and London, and this is the initial investment to buy a factory here in Swansea. We supply the American Space Agency and Neil Armstrong, the astronaut, will be opening the new factory for us. So there will be large press coverage and as we will be looking for banking facilities, perhaps you would like to attend the opening ceremony and start to build a relationship with my staff, including Ms Davenport here, who is our financial director,' said Morris, looking at Sarah. *Boy, am I enjoying this*, he thought.

Boy, is he overdoing it, thought Sarah.

'Create an account straight away for Mr…er… I didn't catch your name, sir, I'm sorry.'

'Leyland – Mark Leyland, Imperial Clothing Industries, or ICI. You've probably heard of us.'

'Yes, of course,' said the manager. 'Exchange the Irish notes for sterling, George.'

After George calculated the exchange rate and passed over the notes, Mark and Sarah left the bank telling the manager to expect an invitation to meet Neil Armstrong in the post.

Chapter 21

Morris and Sarah left the bank. It was late afternoon and they were hungry, so they headed towards a cafe and ordered fish and chips.

When they finished eating they looked at each other without saying anything; knowing their time together was nearly over.

'I've been in touch with Daddy and we've arranged to meet at a secret location. He's arranged for me be picked up from the main railway station in Birmingham,' said Sarah.

'Oh,' said Morris. 'I will need to get home to water my houseplants. It's been a long time.'

'Only four days,' said Sarah, 'and your wife will want to see you.'

Morris's mouth opened instinctively. 'How did you know I had a wife?' he queried.

'Just a guess,' said Sarah.

'Oh,' said Morris. 'I didn't mean to lie to you, but we were on such an adventure. It seemed appropriate for me to be single.'

'I understand, and if you weren't married I wouldn't be leaving tonight. You're kind, considerate, funny and heroic,' said Sarah.

No one had ever said so many kind words to Morris. He was just 'Mr Ordinary' for most of his life.

'I'll take you to the station, then,' he said.

They walked to the car knowing this would be the last time they would see each other.

He stopped at the station and opened the car door. She stood in front of him.

'When we were in the hotel room, I was standing before you naked and I wanted you, Morris. I wanted you to hold me and feel our bodies close through the night. I feel safe in your arms.'

Morris looked down at the pavement about to say something but didn't. He looked up and held the gold chain in his fingers before kissing her full on the lips. As he pulled away, he said, 'I love—'

She put her fingers to his mouth. 'Shh…better not say it. Bye, Morris.'

In a suitcase bought from Kings, Goodman and Baker she had packed all her possessions; somewhat less than when they met four days ago.

After watching her walk up the steps, he turned around and kicked a tyre on his car. He then started the engine and headed home. Driving through the night along the A4 to Reading, he turned off towards the village of Pangbourne. The journey seemed to be a dream as Morris could only think of the last four days and his beloved Sarah. He stopped once and bought fuel and sandwiches. As he drove, he smiled and felt empowered recollecting how he'd dealt with international kidnappers, the IRA, rowing a boat and thinking on his feet when confronted with desperate situations. All alongside a beautiful girl he had fallen in love with, and who had fallen a little in love with him.

Listening to Radio 3 on the car radio, he started to hum to himself as he drove into Willow Avenue. It was very late and most of the inhabitants had gone to bed.

Morris opened the door as quietly as possible and went to the kitchen to make a cup of Horlicks after which he slowly ascended the stairs and entered the bedroom.

He could hear the heavy breathing of Penelope. He went over and kissed her on the cheek. 'Hello, love,' he said.

Penelope opened her eyes in shock. *Love, he never calls me 'love'. How sweet.* 'Have a good trip, dear?' she said rolling over.

'Oh, the usual. Sold a bit and changed the car.'

'That's nice.' She rolled back over again.

Morris undressed and climbed into bed and lay there looking at the reflection of the street light on the ceiling. 'I might play bowls on Sunday.'

'That's nice, dear, you can relax with your friends. You deserve it. Night.'

The next morning Morris woke early. He went downstairs, made a cup of tea and some toast, and took some up to Penelope, all the while whistling an unrecognisable tune.

Penelope thought, *he's in a good mood. He must be glad to be home.*

That Sunday Morris played bowls, and everyone remarked how good he was playing. There was a new sort of confidence about him. After the game he sat and had tea with the other players. He was the centre of attention as he recounted how Telford was a growing town, Chester had a great history dating back to the Roman occupation, and then Dublin, and Cork, and so on – interesting trip selling ladies' clothing, nothing unusual.

Chapter 22

Monday morning and Morris phoned Mr Squires to arrange a visit at head office in Harrogate the next day.

Morris said goodbye to Penelope late afternoon and headed north. He stayed in a bed and breakfast and arrived at the office nine o'clock the next morning.

The receptionist greeted him and welcomed him back before taking him into Mr Squires.

'Ah, Morris, my boy. How are you? Sit down.'

Morris sat opposite Mr Squires looking over an enormous mahogany desk. In fact, the whole room was a throwback to when Squires was a great business and the office was a reminder of those days.

'It sounds as if the trip went well, Morris. Tell me about it,' said Mr Squires.

Morris smiled and thought, *if I told you the truth, you wouldn't believe it.* 'Well there was a good order from Ashford's in Telford, and KGB in Swansea. In Dublin I met an Indian importer, not an importer of Indians, but an importer who was an Indian, and he took a large order paying in cash. I have the money right here in Irish pounds and when the order was ready, I said that I would deliver them myself. He liked the idea of personal service.'

Mr Squires looked in amazement as Morris stacked one hundred and fifty Irish pounds on the desk.

'Well done, Morris. What a success. Look, I've been thinking things over with my wife. I'm not a young man any more and the business is not as buoyant as it used to be, so my wife and I decided we would like you to take over the running of the company. Bring it into the twentieth century. You're a good salesman, understand modern techniques, and things known as computers are getting more popular for running a business with specialised gloveware.'

'Software,' said Morris.

'Whatever. What do you think? Would Penelope move up here to the north? Of course it would be more money, but we can't hold out much longer. Could you turn it around, Morris?'

'Well, I have ideas about extending the range, catalogues and importing goods. It's so much more profitable than home-made goods, and then there's television.'

'Good, Morris, good. When can you start?'

'In two weeks? I need to resign my various clubs down south and put the house on the market. I will probably rent somewhere until the house is sold, so Penelope can stay there in the interim.

'Two weeks! Eh, wonderful. Welcome aboard,' said Mr Squires.

Chapter 23

Morris moved to Harrogate and stayed in a hotel until he found a house becoming of a man who was now managing director of a progressive company. It was the early 70s and the world was changing rapidly with communications and technology.

The rest of the world looked to the United Kingdom for fashion, music and technological advances; Morris was going to embrace them all.

Penelope settled into her new environment and made friends at the cribbage club where she played three times a week. She was even having golf lessons, as Morris thought this would be good for their image.

Morris had a plan to bring the name of Squires into the modern era. It meant a new logo, new clothing range and a new catalogue. Soon the whole of the UK would know the name Squires as a byword for quality at reasonable prices. To achieve this quickly Morris had to find new suppliers and designers, so he went along to the local college and put forward the idea of a new clothing range for Mr and Mrs Average. The student with the best design would be taken on permanently at Squires. To get the college to agree he had to put up a sizeable sponsorship fee, which he did by convincing the bank he was going to revolutionise the company. It would become a brand as popular as St Michael's, Littlewoods and Burtons. Morris took the chance to speculate to accumulate with the bank's money. He travelled to India and the Far East to make contact with manufacturers from all regions offering a full range of clothing items for men, women and children.

The successful student was a girl called Georgina who was nineteen years old and had wonderful ideas for free-flowing dresses, trousers, and exotic colours for women and men alike. This was the age of flower power and the world listened to whatever sounds and designs were coming out of the UK: the Beatles, Cat Stevens, Jimi Hendrix, Mary Quant and Vivien Westwood. Everybody dressed like Sgt Pepper, and Georgina understood this – in addition to the sort of clothes her mum and dad might wear.

Chapter 24

Morris took Georgina to India to understand how vibrant colours in smooth silk made people feel free and happy. The back streets of Bombay were a labyrinth of small businesses manufacturing anything they could that would sell to rich western countries. They saw colours, which they'd never seen in northern England, in opulent fabric worn by Indian women who could barely afford to feed their children.

They stayed in the Bombay Majestic Hotel, which was a throwback to when the British ruled India. On one trip Morris took Georgina out for a meal in an upmarket restaurant where he discussed the future of Squires over various curry-flavoured foods.

'I want you to look at these fabrics tomorrow, Georgina, and imagine how we can introduce them into a range to suit British tastes. We will bring out a catalogue, but more important we will feature them in a new TV advert for ITV – the first of its kind. There will be music, flowers, pretty girls and boys,' said Morris.

Georgina understood what Morris was aiming for. She started drawing on a napkin what she had in mind: kaftans, bell-bottomed trousers and silk scarves.

Georgina was a Newcastle girl with a pretty tough upbringing. Falling foul of the law with drugs and drink, she never found her forte until going to college and joining the fashion department where she was able to express her artistic side. She was straight talking, pretty in a tomboy sort of way and had a scorpion tattoo on her neck.

'Why the scorpion?' said Morris whilst fingering his glass of wine.

Georgina was taken by surprise as Morris was her boss and this seemed quite an intimate question. 'Oh, it's…hmm… Just a design, I suppose,' she said.

'But why a scorpion, and not perhaps a butterfly? he asked, trying to sound worldly.

'Well,' said Georgina, 'I've worked for you the last six months and you haven't noticed anything different?'

'Not to my knowledge,' said Morris, now intrigued.

'Oh,' said Georgina, 'well, one doesn't handle a scorpion. In other words keep off – especially men.'

Morris looked at the wine glass and tried to figure out what she was saying. 'Ah, I see, you prefer women's company – take holidays on the Isle of Lesbos, et cetera.'

'You got it, Boss,' said Georgina.

'Well, each to his or her own.'

Morris had never become involved in the world of homosexuals and lesbians. They were always other people, not in his circle, but he thought that everyone should have the freedom to love who they like. His mind wandered back to Sarah and their close relationship, her porcelain white body, her intellect and piano playing. *Will we ever meet again?* he pondered.

As his mind wandered through the past, Georgina coughed and said, 'Well, it's late and I've got a busy day tomorrow, so it's time for bed.'

'Oh, yes, of course,' said Morris. 'We're leaving in the evening, so see you back at the hotel at five o'clock.'

'Right, Boss,' said Georgina.

'You can call me Mor… No, it doesn't matter. Goodnight.'

'Goodnight, Boss, and thank you.'

She walked from the restaurant back to the hotel. Morris paid the bill and followed. As she was walking along the street, bustling with bikes and taxis, Georgina was suddenly approached by a gang of three young men somewhat worse for drink. They followed Georgina until they reached a dark alleyway and bundled her into the dark recess.

Morris, who was fifty yards behind, ran to the alleyway and saw the men holding Georgina up against the wall. Her cries couldn't be heard above the busy street, so Morris rushed at the gang and told them to leave her alone. They laughed and two of them turned on Morris.

The one holding Georgina against the wall began to tear at her shirt while Morris was being held back by the other two.

'Look, you fools, the scorpion on her neck – don't you know that's a sign of a leper? In Germany they brand all lepers with a scorpion to warn people off,' shouted Morris.

The young man pinning her against the wall saw the scorpion and yelled before stepping back. The other two released Morris, looked at each other and ran as fast as they could back into the street amongst the milling crowds.

Morris took Georgina in his arms and quickly pulled her shirt across her chest.

'I'm so sorry. So sorry,' said Morris.

'For what?' said Georgina. 'Quick thinking?'

'For bringing you here and seeing you violated in this way.'

'I come from Newcastle, remember, and it's not the first time. Why do you think I prefer women? But I must admit, with guys like you around I might change,' she said, laughing.

'You just be as you are and keep thinking fabrics,' said Morris. 'I'll arrange to have an escort with you tomorrow for protection while I'm visiting factories.'

'No damage done. Just a button missing. Thank you again, Mor... Sorry, Boss, you're a hero.'

Once again Morris was hailed a hero; it brought back all the memories of his glory days fighting the KGB and IRA with

Sarah. He felt empowered and put his arm around Georgina. 'Come on, back to the hotel for stiff drink.'

'I'm with you there, Boss!'

They quickly returned to the hotel a little dishevelled but calm. Georgina felt safe with Morris, the Boss Man, and he felt like a father figure. They sat at the bar where Morris told Georgina how he became Managing Director of Squires following a successful sales trip to Ireland.

'Do you ever look at church towers?' Morris said absentmindedly.

'Well, actually, no.'

'Well, they're fascinating. The different building styles and intricate stonework, the stone facings and use of materials, and how it varies from one part of the UK to another. How some churches had spires built taller than the next town just as a status symbol. The craftsmen working for a pittance creating beautiful features for generations to come and admire.'

'It must've passed me by when growing up in Newcastle,' said Georgina, letting out a loud yawn.

'It's late, we must go to our rooms,' said Morris.

They entered the lift to the sixth floor and walked down the corridor where they had adjacent rooms.

'Goodnight, Boss,' said Georgina before giving Morris a peck on the cheek. 'You're OK.'

'Er, goodnight, and I'm sorry again.'

Georgina smiled and let herself into her room.

Morris unlocked his door and switched on the light. After pouring himself a whisky he flopped on the bed. The noise from the street below resounded up into the sky. Morris lay there looking at the fan going round and round.

Do lesbians ever change back, he thought to himself, *assuming being heterosexual was normal and homosexuality was a passing phase.* Like most of the male species, Morris couldn't comprehend two men having sex – it repulsed him. Yet two women, in his imagination, seemed OK – softer, more loving.

Morris imagined Georgina knocking on the door and entering his room wearing just a silk dressing gown holding a bottle of champagne. He closed his eyes and his mind continued to work his imagination. Morris saw Georgina standing at the foot of the bed with her body half lit from the streetlight. Her full body reminding him of the Venus de Milo, but her arm was missing and he saw the sign of the scorpion on Venus's neck. He suddenly woke and realised it was just a dream.

Just then there was a light knock on the door; he thought his dream was coming true.

'Just a moment,' said Morris. He tucked in his shirt and went to the door – the blood rushing through his veins.

'Good evening, sir. I'm sorry to trouble you, but you left your wallet on the bar,' said a uniformed bellboy.

'Oh, thank you, thank you very much. Here, take this.' Morris gave the boy a very large gratuity.

Morris shut the door and went to the bathroom. He looked in the mirror and first saw Morris Bridges the man from Willow Avenue – a shy, inconsequential sort of guy. Guilt does that to a man. Then he looked again and saw Morris Bridges, Managing Director of Squires International, successful businessman, friend of politicians and world leaders, and donor to the Conservative Party.

'Which do you want to be, Morris?' he said to himself with a smile. He then undressed and went to bed.

The next morning he went down to breakfast and saw Georgina already sitting at a table on her own eating a lot of muesli and fruit.

'Morning, how are you?' he asked.

'I'm fine, but when I lay in bed last night I recalled the mugging in the street and what could have happened if you weren't there to rescue me. I suddenly wanted some warmth and strong arms around me – silly me.'

Oh bugger, thought Morris. 'Right, I've arranged for a porter to take you around. Be careful and come back with some beautiful creations. Here's the equivalent of one hundred pounds in rupees, keep it well hidden. Good luck see, you at five.'

'Leave it with me, Boss,' she said leaving the table.

Morris ate alone thinking, *'wanted some warmth and strong arms around me'. But whose arms?*

Morris spent the day visiting factories while Georgina combed retail outlets to find inspiration to take back to the UK. They met in the lobby of the hotel at five o'clock and caught a taxi to the airport.

A porter started to take their luggage on a trolley. As Georgina walked beside him, he looked across and saw the scorpion tattoo.

'Ahhhh,' he screamed, running off waving his arms in the air.

'What the hell was all that about?' said Morris.

'Goodness knows. He looked across at me and yelled something like "cody".'

'Cody? What does that mean?' he said.

Just then a distinguished Indian gentleman approached them. 'May I help,' he enquired. 'I saw the young man run off shouting.'

'Yes,' said Georgina, 'he looked at me and said "cody" before he ran off waving his arms.'

'Cody,' said the gentleman, 'what on earth. Ah, "kodhee" is Hindu for leper. He thinks you are a leper, but I don't think so – are you?'

'Of course not,' said Georgina. 'Thank you for your help, we'll be all right now.'

As the Indian gentleman left, Morris smiled at Georgina. She looked at him quizzically. 'What's amusing you?'

'Turn this way.'

Georgina turned around bemused.

'Ah yes,' said Morris, 'the scorpion, the sign of the leper. That porter must've been one of the thugs who attacked you last night and believed my story about the scorpion.'

Georgina burst out laughing. 'I told you, it protects me from undesirables, especially men.'

Morris pushed the trolley to the check-in desk, and then they went to the executive class waiting room for coffee and sandwiches.

'I really feel good in your company, Boss,' said Georgina. 'Whatever happens to me, you come to my rescue – my hero.'

Oh no, not again, thought Morris. *I can't go on being Superman. After all, I'm Morris Bridges, ex-ladies' underwear salesman.*

Chapter 25

The flight was a night-time schedule, and they settled into their business class seats looking forward to the executive service. One hour into the flight, after the food was cleared away, Morris asked Georgina what sort of day she'd had looking for fabrics.

She reached into her bag and pulled out swatches of colourful materials. 'I think I could design a whole range based on these authentic Eastern patterns. Not only for women but men as well. We need an endorsement from a celebrity to start wearing these clothes on TV.'

'I met Lionel Blair once,' he mocked.

'Hardly a fashion icon. No, we need a pop group or actor. Someone who's seen a lot. The Rolling Stones or Bay City Rollers, for example.'

'Pardon,' said Morris. 'I'm not familiar with their work,' he said teasing. 'I'll work on it when we get back. I know a few show business friends.'

They talked in whispers as fellow travellers were beginning to settle down for the long flight back to Heathrow. Soon Georgina began to yawn. She pulled a blanket up over her knees and was soon in a deep sleep.

Morris never slept on planes. He told people if the plane crashed he wanted to be fully aware of the consequences – usually death – so he was reassured.

While Georgina was sleeping she moved over towards Morris, slipped her arm through his and rested her head on his shoulder.

Morris could feel her closeness and settled down to make her comfortable. He slept in fits and starts making sure his companion was covered with the blanket. He stroked a hair away from her eyes and thought the Morris of old would never know what to do, but Superman Morris seemed at ease doing what he was now doing, naturally.

They touched down at Heathrow, caught the train into London King's Cross and booked first-class tickets to Harrogate.

'I like travelling with the boss, it makes me feel real posh,' said Georgina.

'Only the best for my staff,' said Morris feeling proud of turning Squires around to become a leading name in clothing.

He left Georgina in Harrogate and caught a taxi to his house, which was befitting a man of substance. He opened the front door and called out, 'Penny! Penny!' There was no reply.

He dropped his suitcase in the hallway and made his way through to the garden where he saw Penelope on the terrace overlooking the vast lawn. She was wearing a large floppy hat and dark glasses and holding a pair of binoculars.

'I didn't realise you were interested in birdwatching, my love. A new hobby?'

'Hello, darling. Yes, so many birds... Oh, look there's a sparrow,' she quickly added.

Morris looked at the sparrow. *Big deal,* he thought. Then his eyes were diverted further down the lawn where he could see the swarthy figure of Robin, the gardener, showing the top half of his muscular torso.

'Oh, I see. There's a Lesser Spotted Robin,' said Morris, feeling clever with himself.

'How was your trip with, er, Georgina, isn't it? Pretty girl with short hair, I remember,' said Penelope.

'Oh fine. We have some wonderful fabrics and hope to bring out a new range within weeks.'

'Stay in the same hotel, did you?'

'Well, yes, of course,' said Morris. *Should I tell her about the attempted mugging? Perhaps not.*

'I hope you weren't too familiar with her. It's not good for staff morale, you know.'

'No, strictly business. Anyway, she bats for the other side.'

'Oh, keen cricketer, is she. Who does she play for?'

'No, I mean she prefers muffins,' said Morris, trying to stop the conversation.

'Is she a baker's daughter?'

'No, she prefers women's company.'

'Oh, does she play bridge?' said Penelope being deliberately obtuse.

'Forget it. Any calls while I was away?'

'The golf club want to know if you would be interested in being nominated for captain next year. Apparently they're desperate.'

'Wow. Of course – what an honour. I'll give them a ring. Any other calls?'

'Mr Squires sent a postcard from Cyprus basically saying keep up the good work and he read about your speech to the CBI in the *Financial Times* – he's very impressed. So he bloody should be the dividends he keeps taking out of the company.'

'That's all?' asked Morris, pouring himself a large whisky.

'Yes. Oh no, and a call from Sarah Davies.'

'David,' corrected Morris.

'You know her, then?'

'Vaguely. Runs a music scholarship at Liverpool Uni. Probably wanting sponsorship,' said Morris blushing heavily and turning away. 'How's the gardener? Did he manage to clear the wood at the bottom?' he said, trying to change the subject.

'She said she met you in Ireland,' said Penelope in an accusing tone.

Morris gulped before saying, 'Ireland, Ireland. Oh, five years ago. Yes, met her on the ferry and we chatted about music, but I explained Squires wasn't a big company. She's probably seen the name on TV recently or in the shops and put two and two together.'

'She asked if you had a good meeting with Neil Armstrong, of astronaut fame. I said I wasn't aware you'd met him, and Miss Davies—'

'David.'

'Sarah David laughed and put the phone down.'

'Very strange,' said Morris. 'Did she leave a number because I might be able to sponsor a scholarship now.'

'I don't think so, Morris!'

'Bugger,' he whispered under his breath.

'Another drink, dear?' offered Penelope. 'You looked flustered.'

'Jet lag. I'll go and lie down for a bit.' Morris left the terrace bewildered. *Why had Sarah phoned?*

Chapter 26

The next day Morris had breakfast, kissed Penelope on the cheek and drove his Jaguar Mark 2 down the driveway through the iron gates and into Harrogate. His mind was preoccupied.

He pulled into the executive car park space and raced up the stairs greeting everybody he saw without barely noticing them. He went straight to his office, closed the door and looked up the number of Liverpool University.

'Oh, hello,' said Morris. 'I'm trying to trace a Sarah David in your music department.'

'Sorry, sir, we have nobody here of that name.'

'Oh, I'm sorry to have troubled you.'

Next he phoned Liverpool General Hospital.

'Excuse me, do you have a nurse called Sarah David working there?'

'I will check, sir.' A few moments elapsed before the operator said, 'I'm sorry, sir. No one here of that name. Someone does remember a Sarah David about five years ago, but she left. Not sure where she went. Very promising girl apparently, I'm sorry.'

'OK, thanks.'

Morris sat there looking at the ceiling when he was interrupted by his personal assistant.

'Welcome back Mr Bridges, just to remind you that you have a manager's meeting at ten o'clock and at noon you're lunching with the Minister of State for Business and Industry.'

'Thank you, Elizabeth. Is Georgina in this morning?'

'Yes, sir, she's showing the design team the fabulous silks you saw in Bombay. She seems very happy and positive and the trip has revitalised her thinking. She seems, I don't know, friendlier.'

'Could you arrange for her to come and see me at four o'clock?'

'Certainly,' said Elizabeth.

Morris looked at the sales figures for the various company components of Squires' shops and catalogue. Everything seemed to be booming. He looked at the balance sheet and decided it was time they got into sponsorship.

It was ten o'clock and time for the meeting.

'Good morning, ladies and gents. I trust you've been working hard in my absence. Rod, I want you to look at more locations for retail, possibly another four shops – two in the south and two in Ireland.'

'Ireland?' Rod look surprised. 'What about the troubles?'

'Try Dublin and Cork, they might be joining the Common Market in the next three years and money will be pouring into the Republic.'

'Good thinking, sir,' said Anna from marketing.

Creep, thought Morris. 'Right, I want to discuss a new venture for the group and that is sponsorship in its many forms. I want the six of you to look at your particular area and see where we might get most exposure. For instance, Mike, sportswear, look at major sporting events. Wimbledon, FA Cup, the Derby, that sort of thing – big-time events.'

'Will do,' said Mike.

'Anna, retail, look at large developments. Shopping centres, arcades or malls, as the Americans call them.'

'OK,' said Anna.

'Rod, overseas development, look at foreign companies holding exhibitions in the main arenas in this country and whether Squires could be a sponsor.'

'Leave it with me,' affirmed Rod.

'Richard, finance, see if we can tie up with a bank to co-host high profile events. For example, rock concerts. I believe the Rolling Stones and Beatles are very popular, and The Bachelors and Val Doonican in Ireland.'

'Yes, of course,' said Richard.

'Rachel, you're the figures whizz kid. Look at costs, benefits and profit.'

'No problem,' she answered.

'Fred, music, I want you to look into classical music. Last Night of the Proms, though the BBC have that tied up, so no advertising there. But other major concerts, especially up-and-coming musicians who may hit the big time and need a little financial help on the way. I believe there are several young Russian pianists entering the UK. Investigate thoroughly and come back with some names.'

'Look forward to it,' said Fred.

'This is an exciting diversion for Squires but with television now very popular, we must make the Great British public aware that Squires may have started in ladies' underwear but are now the leading brand for the modern Mr and Mrs. We've cracked it. You might say no, that's probably not the best term to use, but go to it and come back in a fortnight with a broad picture where we can get the best exposure.'

There were murmurs and shuffling as everyone collected up their paperwork and files.

'Fred, I'm particularly keen to pursue classical music. Find out what you can. What about that guy who defected to the west years ago with so much publicity, Davidovic? What's he doing now?' Morris closed his folder abruptly and the managerial staff left the boardroom full of excited chatter.

'Gosh, he is forward thinking.'

'See you at Wimbledon!'

'Ireland, eh?'

'In the Common Market...' and off they went to their respective desks.

Morris returned to his office and buzzed the intercom. 'Elizabeth, request the chauffeur bring the car round in fifteen minutes and take me to the Grand Hotel.'

A short while later Morris was sat in the back of the black limousine driven by long-time employee Alf Reynolds. In fact Alf had driven Mr Squires around in the infamous Rover, which Morris somehow lost in Ireland.

'I loved that car, Mr Bridges, and I expect you did, too. What a shame it was blown up in Cork. Bet you're glad you weren't in it! *Boom!*'

'It certainly saw a lot of action,' said Morris thinking back to the various car chases, the accident in the Merc, and when he became superhuman and thought he'd killed one KGB agent and stunned another with a piece of wood. But worst of all, he shot a cow. He smiled as he recalled the adventure and, of course, saving Sarah. *From who knows what?* pondered Morris.

'Grand Hotel, Mr Bridges,' said Alf.

'Good, pick me up at two.'

Morris entered the grandiose foyer with a marble staircase and glass chandeliers.

A young lady approached him. 'Mr Bridges? My name is Christine, I'm the minister's PA. He is waiting in the restaurant for you.' Christine led Morris through the double glass doors where he was greeted by the manager.

'Good afternoon, sir. Your table is in the recess and the gentleman is waiting for you.'

'Ah, Morris,' said Sir Richard, 'good to see you again. Sit down. How is the fastest growing business in the north doing?'

'Very well. I've just returned from India where we have purchased a range of fabrics to produce a new range in our factory in Harrogate. All exciting stuff.'

'Look, Morris, order your food, and I'll come straight to the point.'

Morris glanced at the menu, ordered and turned towards Sir Richard who seemed a little hesitant.

'Morris, the PM appreciates the help you've given to the party's coffers, heaven knows we need it, and because you've been so successful in business we want you to head a new task force to promote the UK and its business opportunities. What with the PM getting animated about joining the Common Market we need a successful face to head the campaign, and we think you're the man. Get it right and there's probably a knighthood in it for you. You can have an office in London and staff, and we will give you a budget to work with. It means high profile meetings, TV interviews and pictures in the papers. What do you say?'

Morris's fork full of salmon stopped motionless halfway to his mouth. *Sir Morris Bridges or Lord Bridges of Harrogate.* Morris blinked and came back to the words of Sir Richard.

'Well, I could probably give you two days a week for six months, but Squires always comes first.'

'Of course, of course. Would you like "By Appointment to HM The Queen" on your stationery? I can fix that. Just give her couple of tweed jackets and a blanket for the corgis and you're in.'

'I don't suppose she will wear one of our multi-coloured kaftans in a TV advert?' said Morris.

Sir Richard burst out laughing. 'Good man, Morris. You're the type this country needs more of – not these young socialist whippersnappers straight out of university with no knowledge of life.'

Morris finished his meal, shook hands with the minister and left the hotel.

Alf was waiting for him outside. 'Good meeting, sir?' he asked.

'Oh, yes, Alf. Oh yes.' Morris settled back in the seat; even a drab day looked great on the journey back to the office.

At four o'clock Georgina knocked on his door.

'Come in. Ah, Georgina. Recovered from your trip to India?'

'Yes, Mr Bridges, and thank you again – you restored my faith in men, but enough of that. I've been going through the fabrics, and we've come up with some designs that should appeal to the public. Look, here are some rough sketches.'

Morris glanced through the drawings of brightly coloured dresses, coats and shirts. He could see the country needed these patterns to embrace the movement of 'flower power' and 'free love' led by the music and arts industry.

'Very exciting, Georgina,' said Morris. 'Get the final designs to the factory and arrange a fashion show that's going to hit the press and TV. Let's bring colour into this drab world. You've done well. I want you to be part of the expansion of Squires.'

'No more travel for a while Mr Bridges?' said Georgina.

'You can call me Morris when we're alone.'

'Oh, thank you, er...Morris.'

Chapter 27

Three weeks passed by and the new range was ready to be shown. Meanwhile Morris spent a couple of days in London and was given an office in Victoria with five staff. He started to draw up a plan to promote the United Kingdom in its bid to enter the Common Market.

When he returned to Harrogate, Morris called a meeting of the six department managers to discuss how the sponsorship deals were looking.

'Rod, overseas, what have you got?'

'Well, sir, foreign car manufacturers see a big market in the UK and will be forming a network of dealers and looking to work with established British companies in joint sponsorship.'

'I didn't spend four years up to my knees in muck and bullets fighting the bloody Germans to go and buy their cars,' said Morris joking. Of course he didn't – he was in catering. 'Good. Mike, sports?' he continued.

'Well, the euphoria of winning the World Cup in '66 has died down, but domestic football is getting a bigger audience and TV coverage. So there is scope with any major team sponsoring shirts, cars, ground advertising, et cetera, and this applies to motor racing and horse racing.'

'Sounds promising.'

Anna and Richard put forward fairly banal comments, but Morris wanted to hear what Fred had to say regarding classical music. 'And you, Fred, any luck?'

'Yes, Mr B. As tapes and record players are gaining in popularity so is classical music, and the scene in London with shows like *Hair the Musical* is very buoyant, so there is scope. Pop music is dominated by the major record companies, and it's very difficult find groups and singers who are independent.'

Get to classical music for God's sake, man, Morris thought to himself.

'Rock concerts would embrace sponsorship, but the image of drug taking and alcohol is not for Squires, I think,' continued Fred. 'We want punters clothed in Squires' stuff.'

Stop babbling man, thought Morris impatiently.

'And classical music has an outlet, though the view is nothing too vulgar. Soft backing as opposed to sponsorship, I call it. There are a number of talented musicians coming from Japan, mostly violin, and a few Eastern Europeans breaking into the international concert scene. You asked specifically about Joseph Davidovic who now lives in this country. His latest composition "Water Mountain Sky" is proving very popular on the radio and it's challenging pop music in the charts. It is a full orchestra but mostly a piano played by a relatively new young pianist – I haven't as yet found out the name of this artist.'

'You must do so,' ordered Morris in a threatening tone to the astonishment of the others. 'I think our image will be enhanced with this genre of music.'

'But it's hardly Mr and Mrs Average, is it, sir?' said Mike who wanted to go down the sports route.

'It will be, Mike, believe me. There'll be radio stations dedicated entirely to the great composers and the Great British public will be buying more classical music. I think, though, to give an even balance, we should concentrate on popular sports, football probably. Let's sponsor a first division team and have Squires emblazoned on the shirts. Also, for balance, let's go for selected classical music. Thank you. Go away and come back with some details. Fred, stay a moment, will you?'

Fred stayed seated as the others left the room.

'Fred, I want you to try and trace Joseph Davidovic.'

'I understand because he defected from Russia some years ago he's quite reclusive, although things are somewhat easier with the Eastern bloc now, but he remains out of the spotlight,' replied Fred.

'Find out if there is family and where they are and, Fred, go down town immediately and buy the tape of "Water Mountain Sky" or an album and bring it back to me.'

Morris sat back in his chair and looked across the grey rooftops and chimneys of industrial Harrogate. Not the bit the tourists saw; they saw municipal gardens and the arcade of shops and of course Betty's Tea Rooms.

He felt his heart beating faster as he believed, perhaps, he was once again getting closer to his beloved travelling companion. But now he *really* was like his alter ego Mark Leyland, friend of the spacemen. He was successful, wealthy, revered and soon to be in the news.

Chapter 28

The new range of clothing proved to be very successful with everyone wearing colourful, sweeping baggy trousers, tops and kaftans. Morris promoted Georgina to head designer where she was free to incorporate her ideas at will.

Morris spent more time in London at his office and government-sponsored flat in Chelsea. He met with members of Parliament, top civil servants and royalty. He became part of the establishment and was instrumental in leading negotiations to enter the Common Market.

He was being quoted in the press and newsrooms, and an interview was set up with the hard-hitting journalist Robin Day, the grand inquisitor. Morris performed well defending the government's decision to enter Europe despite much opposition. Although the general public knew very little about the Common Market, they assumed the government knew what it was doing.

Meanwhile Penelope was getting on with her life playing golf and cribbage, and admiring Robin – now a regular visitor – and his hollyhocks. Since playing golf and attending the local spa, Penelope had lost weight, updated her hairstyle and received advice on make-up. She was quite an attractive middle-aged woman who seemed to float around the house and garden in long, flowing silk gowns, dark glasses and a Martini in her hand.

Morris, of course, hadn't really noticed a change in Penelope as he was too busy being a man of importance.

***

Two months passed by and Morris called in on Fred to check if he'd had any success finding musical talent who required sponsorship. Fred informed him that a violinist from Japan was causing a lot of attention and perhaps a concert or two sponsored by Squires would be productive.

'And Davidovic?' asked Morris casually.

'Well, you can't get near him, and he declines all contact with the press. But his work "Water, Mountain Sky" will be performed at the Manchester Free Trade Hall next month with full television coverage, but we've missed the sponsorship timeslot – not enough time.'

'Get on the phone now and make sure you book me a box. If it's sold out, tell them who it's for – they'll find room. I'm sure they know I'm on the Arts Grants Committee,' said Morris, completely out of character.

Meanwhile, somewhere in southern Ireland, the Reilly family were in the local hostelry. Now the country was going to join the Common Market they felt it the right time to get into construction. There were roads to be built with European money, and it was important the Reillys were in on it.

The bar had a television showing the news. 'And now over to London for an update on the British government joining the Common Market and their spokesman Mr Morris Bridges. Good Evening, Mr Bridges. As you know, the Republic of Ireland is preparing for entry to the Common Market on the same day as the UK, what is your opinion?'

'Holy Mary, it's him! Look, it's him! He stole our money and our car! The black Rover man and the girl!'

'Calm down, Michael. Are you sure now?' said Sean Reilly.

'It's him! It's him!' said Michael.

'Well, well, well. Perhaps we'll be making a trip across the water very soon. A business trip, you might say.'

At the same time in Bulgaria, two Russian men dressed in black were enjoying a meal in a bar in Sophia. A TV was heard in the background whilst they drank beer. They were laughing until one of them choked on his potatoes watching the TV screen.

'Eto on! It is he!' he said gasping and pointing at the screen as the Bulgarian news station reported on the expansion of the European Economic Community. The other Russian looked around and spat out the contents of his mouth on the clean cafe floor.

'Kurvenok! Bastard!' cried the cafe owner.

The two Russians kicked a chair out of their path and lunged for the phone on the wall.

'Kurvenok,' said the owner again.

'Director, we have business in England – er, we have detected a traitor of the state... Good, yes... We will leave immediately.'

Back in London, Fred returned to Morris's office. 'I've booked a box. Who else should I allow for concerning the seats and drinks?'

'Just the one, Fred. Just the one.'

Fred looked astonished. 'It was very expensive, Mr Bridges, are you sure? What about Mrs Bridges?'

'I'm sure, Fred.'

Morris knew Penelope had no interest in classical music. She was more into Sinatra and even Elvis. Penelope was having the house redecorated; Robin, the gardener, was proving to be very adaptable and handy with everything, it seemed.

At the same time, on a terrace overlooking the Mediterranean, Mr Squires turned to his wife and said, 'Just reading about our boy, Morris, in *The Times*. He is very highly regarded in government circles and the Squires' name seems to be everywhere. They're on the red shirts playing Arsenal on Saturday, and he's opening four more shops – even in Ireland. They say he's going upmarket into classical music. When he came back from Ireland five years ago, he seemed to be a changed man – more positive, more dynamic, more awareness.'

'Must've been the water, dear. Pass me my G and T. Shall we take the yacht out tomorrow, perhaps towards Sicily?'

Chapter 29

The day of the concert was here. Morris was excited at the prospect of hearing this magnificent work by Joseph Davidovic performed live. There was one piece that Morris would like to use in his TV advert; he suspected the composer's agent would be there to talk to.

Morris had a routine day in the office after which he went home to shower and put on his evening suit. He packed a holdall and suit bag and told Penelope he would be flying to Dublin after the concert.

'That's nice, dear,' she said.

Penelope had friends over for a game of cribbage. Robin was preparing the finger buffet. *So bloody versatile that guy*, thought Morris. *I could marry him myself.*

He decided to drive himself as he enjoyed the anonymity of the Jaguar and it gave him a chance to put his foot down, but it was a filthy wet evening as he pulled out of the drive. He estimated it would be a couple of hours to reach Manchester, so he decided to take a few back roads to avoid the sprawling towns around Bradford and Leeds. Whilst driving he put on the radio to listen to the six o'clock news.

'Prime Minister Heath told a reporter that negotiations on the Common Market were progressing. Although there were some sticking points, he had full confidence in the team led by Morris Bridges to come out with the best deal for the UK in Europe.'

Morris smiled to himself thinking how far he'd come in the last few years: from selling ladies' underwear to being a friend of the Prime Minister of Britain. Not that the Prime Minister was the most affable of chaps as he was prone to tantrums.

Just as Morris found himself on a lonely stretch of road with the rain pouring down, he saw a parked car ahead with its lights flashing. As he passed by, he saw a figure bent over a body in the road and there was smoke coming from the front of the car.

Oh my God, thought Morris, *a serious accident and someone's hurt*. He stopped and reversed to see a small, slightly built figure shuffling up to the car.

'I'm so sorry, could you help me. I've had an accident and my car is damaged.'

Morris thought it strange to be concerned about his car when there was a dead body in the road. He tentatively got out and walked back towards the scene with the small person.

Morris then recalled the night he picked up Sarah and the trouble he got into then, but his sense of decency said he should help.

'Are they dead?' asked Morris.

'I think so,' said the small person.

As they were approaching the body, it leapt to its feet and ran down the road.

'Jeez,' said Morris.

'Such chutzpah,' said the small man. 'It breaks my car and leaves without saying sorry.'

'So, it was a deer?' questioned Morris.

'Yes, of course. You think a man could run like that?' The small Jewish man was agitated.

'Where were you heading?' asked Morris cautiously.

'Ah, Manchester. But I fear I shall be too late now.'

'I'm going to Manchester. Perhaps I could drop you off in the town, and then you can get a taxi for wherever you're going to.'

They decided to push the damaged car off the road. It was an old Volvo and probably not worth a great deal. They continued the journey and made small talk.

'My name is Joseph, by the way, and thank you for your kindness. You're a good man. You have a heart, but I feel I have seen you before.'

'Perhaps,' said Morris.

'Oh my God,' said Joseph. 'I'm going to a concert in Manchester, and I've left the ticket in the car! What a schmuck!'

'At the Free Trade Hall, by any chance?'

'Why, yes – how did you know?'

'I'm going there myself by coincidence.'

'There is a God after all. But I will not get in without a ticket.'

'Leave it to me,' said Morris.

As they drew up outside the main entrance, two gentlemen approached the car and opened the door.

'Welcome, Mr Bridges. We are so happy to welcome you here this evening,' said the general manager.

'Thank you. Whilst I'm meeting a few people in the bar, could you show this gentleman to my box and give him a stiff drink.'

Joseph stood back open-mouthed, and then he was ushered by staff up the steps into the auditorium and to Morris's box. He sat numbed by what good fortune he was having. *But who is this Samaritan?* he wondered.

Morris glad-handed a few dignitaries in an anteroom from the bar and expressed his pleasure at being in Manchester before going up to his VIP box.

'You are too kind and obviously a man of some importance,' said Joseph.

The lights dimmed down and a hush descended over the hall as the curtains lifted. Immediately the hall broke into applause at the sight of the Hallé Orchestra. First the leader appeared with a violin in hand, followed closely by the conductor.

The conductor turned and smiled at the audience before facing the orchestra. He then glanced to his left, and a young lady in a blue satin dress approached the grand piano. She sat down with her back to Morris and Joseph.

The orchestra started with a great crescendo before being accompanied by the sound of tumbling water from the piano. Joseph nodded his approval.

Morris could see he was conducting with his fingers. The dramatic composition moved throughout the entire movement.

Joseph continued to conduct and give his approval at the piano solo pieces by muttering, 'Good... Good.'

'You know this work remarkably well, Joseph. Do you have a grand piano at home?'

'I know every crotchet and note. After all, I wrote it.'

Morris knocked over his glass of whisky. 'You're...you're Joseph Davidovic?' said Morris.

'Indeed, my boy. I have spent ten long years writing this work and it is the finest I have written. It takes me back to my childhood in Russia, Imperial Russia, where we played in the meadows under the shadow of the mountains. We were poor farmers then, but my parents scraped enough together to send me to the Moscow Conservatory to further my musical education,' he whispered.

The interlude arrived. Morris ordered more drinks – he needed another one, quickly.

Joseph went on to explain that he worked hard at composing and eventually his music was recognised. He played to vast audiences in Moscow and St Petersburg. When the Communist grip was beginning to exert itself on freedom of movement and speech, it became more and more difficult. Then on one cultural exchange he was invited to play at Carnegie Hall in Manhattan, USA.

Whilst in New York he marvelled at the freedom with which people lived their lives and the prosperity that was so obvious, and also that talent in the arts was not only for the wealthy as in Russia. All the time he was there with his wife and daughter for two months playing concerts, he knew he was being monitored by Russian agents everywhere he went.

He wanted so much to stay there in the western world. He discussed it with his wife and they hatched a plan.

The idea was to visit the Empire State Building and take the lift to the top, but beforehand he and his wife were to go shopping in Bloomingdales to buy clothes, lots and lots of clothes. They then travelled by taxi to the Empire State Building. Instead of depositing the large bags with left luggage, they climbed into the lift and took up all the space. When two burly men in suits tried to enter, Joseph said sorry and closed the lift doors before excitedly shouting, 'To the top!' but pressing the button to floor one. They left two guys in grey suits hurriedly looking for a vacant lift, which they found after throwing out an elderly couple, and then they went up to the top floor.

The moment the lift stopped at the first floor, Joseph and his wife grabbed the luggage and hurried outside. They caught a taxi whilst the two minders were on their way to the top of the building – 102 floors higher.

'Where to?' said the cabbie.

'British Embassy, Third Avenue,' said Joseph.

Joseph explained to Morris that the British diplomatic staff took them in and flew them back to the UK by private plane.

'And here I am today, thankfully.'

The lights dimmed and the conductor appeared again. This time the pianist entered from stage right. She smiled at the audience and sat down.

Morris sat there speechless. It was her, his beloved Sarah, in full view with the spotlights picking out a gold chain around her neck.

He turned to Joseph. 'That's Sarah, your daughter, my lo—' He stopped himself before actually saying the word 'love'.

'Now you know why I was desperate to get here, to see her play my work for the first time. She is beginning to be recognised for her beautiful playing, and there's talk of being sponsored by Myers.'

'Squires,' said Morris.

'Yes, whatever.'

They sat back and enjoyed the rest of the concert with Joseph conducting to himself and Morris joining in. The concert ended and there was silence. The conductor turned around and gestured towards Sarah. The audience erupted to cheers and clapping. Sarah faced the auditorium and bowed. As she did, the gold chain fell forward from her neck and sparkled in the spotlights.

'I'm a happy man. If only my wife had been here to witness it, but she passed away. Her spirit is in the music, and I am now content,' said Joseph with tears in his eyes.

The audience continued to applaud and cheer.

Morris said to Joseph, 'Come on, let's go backstage and meet her.'

'I doubt they will let us go there.'

'Leave it to me,' said Morris once again.

Once they reached downstairs Morris found the general manager who, of course, allowed access for his important visitor.

'Of course, Mr Bridges, you can go through to the backstage. What about the other gentleman?'

'This other gentleman is far more important than me. It's Joseph Davidovic, the composer.'

The manager put his hand to his mouth to stop spluttering with surprise. 'Of course, of course. Nigel, show these two gentlemen to the dressing room area.'

They were escorted through dark corridors to the dressing rooms where members of the orchestra were excitedly putting away their instruments into cases. It was quite a push getting through.

Nigel took them straight to the door of the artist and politely knocked on the door.

'Just a moment, I'm not ready yet,' came a female voice.

Morris thought, *she won't be ready for this visitor.* He nearly turned and ran away, so excited was he to be meeting her again.

The door opened. A young lady in sweater and jeans stood there. 'Oh, Papa, how exciting. We did it and they loved it. Where were you sitting?'

'Due to the kindness of this gentleman I had a perfect view. You were outstanding, so much feeling. This is Morris.'

Morris appeared from the half-lit corridor.

At first, Sarah was still putting her dress in a suitcase and didn't look up when she said, 'Oh hello.' She then turned to face him. 'What the hell! It's you, Morris, it's you!' She wrapped herself around Morris's neck.

'You two know each other?' asked Joseph.

'Oh yes, Papa. He is my superhero,' said Sarah.

'The man who took you to Ireland when you were on the run. My God! Sorry, my language, but I'm anglicised now.'

'How about we go for a meal across the road and talk over old times?' suggested Morris.

'You two youngsters go. I'm an old man and tired. I need my rest, and I've got to figure out how to get home.'

Once again Morris said, 'Leave it with me.' He left to make a call and came back a few moments later. 'A car will be waiting for you out the front in fifteen minutes to take you wherever you want to go.'

'Sarah said she had met the kindest man when she was being pursued, and she was right, thankfully. But it has all died down now, and we are free to go where we want,' said Joseph. 'But I still want to keep a low profile and communicate through my music. Now leave, and you look after her, Morris. She's all I've got.'

'I will, sir. I'll never let her out of my life again. Come on, let's go.'

Meanwhile, on the roof of a building opposite, two men in black were looking through their gunsights, fitted with silencers, focusing on the front steps of the Trade Hall. On the other side of the road were two men in balaclavas on the roof looking through their gunsights, fitted with silencers, down at the back steps.

Just as the rooftop assassins were getting ready, they saw a black Jaguar being brought to the front closely followed by a ministerial limousine.

A cat on its nightly scavenge startled a seagull that was settled for the night. It gave a high-pitched squawk as the cat leapt towards it licking its lips.

The screech alarmed one of the men in black who instinctively pulled the trigger on his rifle. Whilst falling backwards, the bullet flew across the street, ricocheted off a flagpole and hit one of the men in balaclavas. This prompted the other man in a balaclava to shoot back.

A hail of bullets ensued from one side to the other for three minutes. Then total silence.

Down in the street below, due to the hustle and bustle of people going home, the traffic noise and horns beeping, no one heard a thing.

Morris and Sarah went into a late-night diner and bought a pizza. By the time they returned to the Jag, all was quiet, bars were closing and street cleaners were going about their business.

They held hands as they crossed the road and got into the car.

'Where shall we go?' said Sarah.

'I've got to open the new store in Cork at the weekend, and we need a celebrity to attract publicity.'

'I'm no celebrity, Morris,' said Sarah.

'You will be. You will be.'

She kissed him on the cheek and said, 'I've missed you.'

Morris looked across and smiled, slightly embarrassed, and thought he'd better talk about something else.

'What do you think about the Common Market?' he asked.

'Well,' she said, 'there was this guy on TV saying if the eight countries worked for a common purpose with trade and services, the whole region of central Europe will benefit and later—'

'Shut up,' said Morris laughing, and they headed to the airport.

At the same time, back in Harrogate, Penelope watched Robin wash the last of the dishes. He was standing at the sink wearing only an apron and rubber gloves.

God, he's so handy, she thought. *If only Morris was as adventurous and attentive as my Robin!*

The End

Printed in Great Britain
by Amazon